# "ABBEY, ABBEY— COME QUICKLY."

*I jumped up and ran to the window in response to the voice I was certain was Charles's, but his name faded on my lips as I realized it couldn't be. Wearily I turned away from the window, when the voice came again much clearer now.*

*"Abbey, Abbey—to the beach."*

*"Who is it?" I called. "Who's there?"*

*Then with a gasp I drew back as the monk appeared, suspended, it seemed, at the cliff edge just as I had seen him the very first time. He had one finger to his lips, then he beckoned to me.*

*"Come, Abbey. Follow me."*

*Without a moment's hesitation, I put on my warmest cloak and stealthily crept out onto the landing.*

*Only when I had turned the corner and saw the glistening frost on the lawns did I wonder what madness had possessed me to follow him into the darkness, perhaps for miles, to the monastery ruins—to THE MONK'S RETREAT.*

# The Monk's Retreat

Susannah Curtis

AVON
PUBLISHERS OF BARD, CAMELOT, DISCUS, EQUINOX AND FLARE BOOKS

Dedicated to the memory of my dear mother, Fanny Gover Beaumont, née Curtis, 1885-1969

Kind acknowledgements to my niece, Margaret Pullen, for her willingness to help, and to my friend, Ann Cooper, for her constant inspiration, also to my fellow writers in the Bournemouth Writers' Saturday Group for their support.

AVON BOOKS
A division of
The Hearst Corporation
959 Eighth Avenue
New York, New York 10019


Published by arrangement with the author.
Library of Congress Catalog Card Number: 76-47860



ISBN: 0-380-00857-2

First Avon Printing, December, 1976

# *One*

## *1839*

THE NIGHT seemed humid and still, and for some reason I was suddenly wide awake.

This wasn't the first time that I had experienced this strange feeling since coming to stay with my sister Emmalina and her husband Greville Bond.

Yet I wasn't actually frightened. The only sound came from the water's edge several feet below the cliff top on which my brother-in-law's house, Castle Grange, stood.

It was a gentle noise at this distance as the water of Lyme Bay lapped, then receded, taking a handful of large pebbles with it each time.

I had been here a month, and learned to love the isolated beach and vast blue sea, especially at dawn when a blue mist hovered, veiling the horizon.

The high neck of my flannel nightgown seemed to be choking me. I felt the need for air, so threw back the bedclothes and slid from the great bed noiselessly, then pushed up the lower half of the tall sash window.

I could hear the rattle of the pebbles more clearly now, and stood briefly before the open window listening to the familiar soothing night sound before climbing back to the comfort of the feather bed.

But still sleep would not come.

Suddenly the heavy curtains were caught in a fierce

draught, and with the screaming wind I was certain I heard a whispered: 'Abbey, Abbey . . .'

Who at this hour of the night could be calling me? Surely not Emma, for she had the protection of her strong husband.

Again I returned to the window, looking out towards the end of the garden where the lawn reached the cliff edge.

I held my breath as for a fleeting second, I caught sight of a shadow, suspended, it seemed, in space where the cliff dropped sheer to the beach below.

I blinked, and the apparition, for surely that was what it must be, had vanished.

The wind died as suddenly as it had arisen, but I closed the window quickly, my body creeping with the cold.

Huddled beneath the sheets, I closed my eyes, but could still see the shadow vividly. The shadow of a figure dressed in a monk's robe and hood!

It must have been dawn before sleep rested my troubled brain and I fear I was somewhat late in putting in an appearance for breakfast.

Emma and Greville had all but finished.

'Why, Abbey, you look quite pale. Have you had a bad night?' Emma asked, as I took my place at table.

'No, Emma,' I replied calmly. 'A little restless. One moment hot, the next quite cold. The air here in Devon is, I fancy, much warmer than farther east along the coast and, I must confess, once I am awake the sound of the sea brings me to life, and I find pleasure in just listening.'

It was a crisp, autumn morning, the trees outside the breakfast room window already beginning to lay their carpet of brown, yellow and red.

Castle Grange dominated many surrounding acres of

fine farmland, owned by the wealthy Greville Bond, a big masculine figure with a long, rugged face, topped with a shock of black hair. Apart from bidding me 'Good morning', he ignored me, as he drank noisily from his large teacup, at the same time reading the morning paper.

So far during my stay here I seldom saw my brother-in-law. He had a farm manager, but preferred, it seemed, to do much of the supervising of his labourers and farmland himself. He was a much feared man, even, I suspected, by his wife, my sister Emma, who in contrast to my nondescript looks was a dazzling beauty, with ringlets of burnished gold, and large soft brown eyes set wide apart in her oval, milky-white face.

We were both of similar medium height, with good figures, but whereas Emma constantly warranted a second look, I had no complimentary features.

My thick, wild hair was of no definite colour, neither dark nor fair, but shone and waved from the vigourous brushing my zealous temper frequently afforded it.

Even though the colour of my eyes changed from grey to green, or green to blue, according to my mood, my one attribute was shrewdness, which, according to my parents, Baron and Baroness Rothesay of Sheridan Lodge in Hampshire, was easily detected in my eyes, and for this reason I was constantly assured no sane man would ever ask for my hand in marriage. Men like their women to be simple but beautiful, I was told.

So, at the age of twenty-two and still without a suitor, my parents had gone to considerable expense to pursue the acquaintance of a certain fat, middle-aged Earl in London.

My shrewdness caused me to anticipate that I should

find no happiness with this man, and, much to my parents' dismay, I refused all the Earl's advances.

The outraged man, no doubt disappointed at the failure of securing a wife, soon set about rumours of the Baroness Rothesay's cold, simple daughter, so I was forced to seek the hospitality of my sister for a while.

This had been easily arranged, for she was looking forward to the birth of her first-born and was grateful for my company through the waiting months, though I felt her gratitude was not shared by her husband.

As always, I had difficulty in satisfying my appetite while Greville sat at the table. He was, in my opinion, uncouth and had coarse eating habits which repelled me.

'What shall we do today, Abbey?' Emma asked.

I laughed. 'I shall take my usual country or seaside walk while you are resting after luncheon,' I told her. 'I should also like to spend an hour or so in the library if I may?'

'You and your books,' Emma chided. 'Of course you may spend as much time in the library as you wish, though I fear the books are old and musty, and there will be little of interest to your tastes.'

'I am interested in the history of Castle Grange,' I explained. 'Indeed in the surrounding parts too, especially the village and its inhabitants. Are there any ghostly stories concerning Castle Rock, I wonder?'

Greville put down his paper and rose from the leather chair.

'If Abbey finds her room distasteful,' he said gruffly 'ask Thwaites to move her to the west wing where it will be quieter.'

'Oh, Grev!' Emma exclaimed. 'The west wing is hardly ever used, it's cold and damp. I'm sure Abbey was not implying she was unhappy on the south side overlooking the sea.'

'Indeed no,' I hastily intervened. 'I love the sea, it's just that—well, I had a strange dream—and thought I saw a ghost, dressed as a monk, so absurd.'

Emma laughed. 'If your ghost visits you again you must have a room on the east side nearer to us.'

'That would never do,' Greville broke in shortly. 'I have to get up at all hours to supervise the estate. I shouldn't like to disturb Abbey unnecessarily.'

Greville Bond didn't appear to be amused by the ghost, and spoke quite severely.

'Really,' I insisted, 'I love the room I'm in. Please don't concern yourselves on my account.'

'But we want you to be happy, don't we, Grev? Even if you are in disgrace in the eyes of the family.'

I felt my colour rising as Greville gave me a leering grin, his long, tarnished teeth protruding between thick lips as he prepared to place his pipe in his mouth.

'Of course we do,' he agreed. 'Make yourself quite at home, though, as Emma said, there's little of interest in the old library.'

So he had taken heed of my wishes to read up the history of Castle Grange, which surprised me.

Emma was not an active person and took a great deal of persuading to walk with me even as far as the cliff edge, where I tried to find some plausible reason for imagining that I had seen a monk there during the night. But there were no trees at the end of the garden, only a crumbling brick wall covered with weeds and ivy.

'Is there no way down to the beach from the garden?' I asked.

'No, only the way you always go, across the meadow and down the lane which leads on to the beach.'

'But what about the east side, Emma? Greville's land stretches right along the cliff edge, does it not?'

'Yes, but the cliff edge is dangerous along there. Surely you must have looked up from the beach and noticed that it's all quite rugged in that direction?'

'Come for a walk with me now, Emma? Let's go exploring?'

Emma laughed. 'In my condition, Abbey, Grev would be most angry. It is most important that I bear him a son, remember. Already he has waited three years.'

'But you need some exercise, Emma. We could go slowly and rest often on the large rocks.'

'You leave your exploring until this afternoon. Here comes Mrs. Thwaites with my needlework basket. I still have plenty to do for the baby, and you never know if it will come early. Wouldn't you like to be in my condition, Abbey? A wealthy husband who gives me all I want, and now a baby?'

'Perhaps, if and when I find the right man,' I told my sister.

'Abigail! As if there is such a thing as the right man! I grant you the Earl was not a great catch as far as looks go, but wealth, such nobility, and no doubt a chance to be presented at Court to the young Queen. Oh, Abbey, do you not feel you were rather too hasty in refusing him?'

'No, Emma, I most certainly do not. Just because you are a little older than me does not mean you can plan my future, as our parents have sought to do. I do not agree on any score with arranged marriages so would be obliged if you would let the matter drop.'

'Grev thinks that although you may not be a stunning beauty you have other qualities more important to a man.' Emma giggled childlishly.

'I don't wish to know what Greville thinks,' I said,

indignantly, and walked away from my sister to sit on the oak seat.

She quickly joined me, and handed me a small white garment to sew.

'Please, Abbey, don't be angry with me for teasing you. We are so very different in temperament and yet get on so well together. I haven't the intelligence you have, I am hopeless at figures, but Grev says he likes me that way. You are always seeking to learn something, always restless to be up and doing, or else with your head buried in a book.'

'That's the way I like to spend my time, Emma. I cannot alter my character. Perhaps I ought to consider taking up some useful profession, like teaching?'

'Oh, Abbey! No. A life of drudgery? Father would never hear of such a thing. The family name of Rothesay would be even more disgraced.'

'I'm sorry you think I have already brought some shame to the family, Emma,' I said, a little hurt. 'I felt that at least as you seem to be happily married you would understand how I felt towards the Earl, a man twice my age, known for his associations wih disreputable women, and for his drinking and gambling.'

'Yes, dear, I do understand, and want you to find contentment as I have done, but I fear there are no eligible bachelors in these parts. After my son is born you must go home and take your place in Society again. There must be other wealthy men anxious to secure a wife from a well-known respectable family.'

I smiled a little to myself as I clumsily threaded the needle with fine silk. Emma could while away the whole day with daydreams as she used her slender fingers to make pretty things, while I craved for the outdoor life, to be walking or riding, whether the sun shone, or the rain fell.

During my first weeks at Castle Grange I had accompanied Emma, sometimes with Greville as well, to visit their friends. On two occasions we had taken tea at the Rectory, where I had learned some of the village gossip. But I did not enjoy making social calls and Emma must have realised this, for I was now frequently left to amuse myself from luncheon until dinner.

I had an agreement with the plump, jolly Mrs. Thwaites, housekeeper of Castle Grange, who, hearing of my long walks and love of the outdoor life took me to the kitchen where she explained to the kitchen staff that I was at liberty to take some refreshment with me on my outings.

Maud, the cook, was Mrs. Thwaites' unmarried sister, a simple country woman with fleshy white hands, strong from the constant kneading of large batches of dough, but with a friendly, pleasant manner.

'You didn't ought to be going too far away today, Miss Abigail,' she said, tossing her head towards the top panes of glass in the kitchen windows, where the only available light entered the huge basement kitchen. 'There's squally showers about and no mistake by the crying of them there seagulls.'

'But it's a beautiful day, Maud. No sign of a cloud anywhere. It's much too good to be shut up indoors,' I told her.

She regarded me disdainfully as she handed me a neatly tied napkin.

'I'll take care, I promise, and at the first sign of a cloud I'll return home,' I assured her with a gratifying smile.

Today I had decided not to go along the beach as my previous inclinations had been. Instead I would go in an easterly direction, but up on the headland in search of some way down to the beach from there.

Crossing the meadow at the front of Castle Grange, I was able to make my way through into the fields which seemed to span for miles upwards and outwards over the deserted headland.

The sea, far below to my right, lay calm, a vast mirror with the sun sparkling like gems on the surface, while overhead large seabirds swooped inland, and then with a mournful cry seemed to let the wind lift them out over the cliff again.

The constant rise of the headland slowed me up considerably, but eventually, though somewhat short of breath, I reached the summit.

The view was truly magnificent, and I sank on to the soft green turf to rest and admire the landscape.

Another headland rose skywards across the valley, and instead of open fields between the two peaks I could see below me an area of dense undergrowth and copseland, where the sea thundered over the rocks in an attempt to meet the waters of the river as it plunged down through the gorge.

As I listened to the reverberating sound my eyes focused on some brickwork peeping between the trees.

Spreading the napkin on the grass beside me, I enjoyed the home-made crusty bread and hunk of cheese supplied by Maud, but found myself curious about the hidden building below. Turning my gaze back the way I had come, Castle Grange was but a dot, austere and lone on the distant horizon.

I felt rested and fortified, and determined to get a closer look at whatever lay at the mouth of the gorge so I ran down the slope towards the trees until I suddenly came upon a stone wall.

This then must be the boundary of Greville Bond's land, but it did not deter me from wanting to see beyond, only there was no way through, and with my long skirt and petticoats I dared not attempt to climb over. I searched for a gate or even a break in the wall, but it appeared well built, so I made my way to the cliff edge.

Here the wall was crumbling, but so was the cliff. It looked a long way down, and yet I felt that the ground upon which I stood was firm enough. Then I noticed a rough pathway on the other side of the wall, leading away under the cliff.

It would be disappointing, having come this far, not to reach the valley, so I decided to try to get over the wall where it had crumbled near the cliff edge. I held on to the jagged stones when a sudden wind blew my skirt up and large drops of rain plopped on to my bonnet. This was no time to be exploring, I thought, remembering Maud's warning.

There seemed to be a foreboding darkness all around me as the sun was blotted out by the inky clouds.

I ran back along the wall, hoping to find some shelter, if only some trees, but there was none. The rain beat down on me, driving me to run and keep running, chasing me away from the cliff edge.

Eventually the ground levelled out and I came to a riding track skirting a pond, on the other side of which I could see cottages.

An arched wooden bridge supplied the only means of access to the cottages, and I was halfway across when a low growl made me stop, and I saw, guarding the other end of the Bridge, a large fearsome-looking bulldog.

I grabbed the rail with one hand and my skirt with the other. He looked at me savagely, his teeth bared ready for attack.

The rain continued to splash on to my face, but I was too terrified to move, or realise that the sound of horse's hooves were rapidly approaching.

Then there was a great shout, a command, and the

bulldog, still eyeing me suspiciously, grunted and turned to waddle off the bridge.

With a sigh of relief I turned to face my rescuer.

He was sitting astride an enormous black stallion. His face, although dripping with water, was wrinkled in a broad smile.

'Charles McClure at your service, Miss . . . ?'

## *Two*

THE COLOUR had drained from my face and my heartbeats were drumming in my ears still, yet as I stared at the handsome weatherbeaten face a serenity calmed me. The drops of rain lessened and, from above, a watery shaft of sunlight descended upon the man, Charles McClure, as he jumped down from his horse.

With a slight bow he raised his hat.

'I don't believe I've had the pleasure of meeting you, Miss . . . ?'

'Rothesay—Abigail Rothesay,' I stammered. 'Thank you for coming to my rescue. I dread to think what might have befallen me had you not arrived when you did. I can't imagine why anyone would allow such a bad-tempered beast to be on the loose.'

He took a step nearer me and a wry smile crossed his face, as he cocked his head to one side to avert my gaze.

'I'm the one to be blamed, Miss Rothesay, for Humphrey is my guard dog.' He tapped one hand lightly with his riding crop.

I was the one now to feel embarrassed, and turning my eyes away from his I mumbled a weak:

'I beg your pardon, sir. But . . .'

'But . . .'

We laughed then as we both spoke together. Above the attractive cleft in his firm square chin, his perfectly shaped lips parted to reveal even white teeth, as his dark brown velvet eyes scanned my bedraggled form.

He was very tall and elegantly groomed in his stylish riding suit.

'But you are very wet, Miss Rothesay. I must apologise if Humphrey frightened you, but he was doing the job expected of him. I doubt that he would have harmed you, but come, let me introduce you properly. Once you're friends you'll be welcome to walk through my land as often as you wish.'

I felt the colour tingeing my cheeks awkwardly as I realised that I must be trespassing.

'Indeed, I'm very sorry,' I began. 'I must confess I was caught at the cliff edge when the downpour came. I had hoped to explore the valley between the headlands, but I did not know to whom the land belongs.'

As we crossed the little bridge, Charles McClure lightly supporting my elbow, tightened his fingers. I quickly glanced towards him and noticed his face was unsmiling now and very grave.

'Have I offended in any way?' I hastened to enquire.

His dark eyes met mine seriously.

'Miss Rothesay, it is not usual for young ladies to wander alone in the countryside. You are safe enough, of course, on your brother-in-law's estate . . .'

'Then you know who I am?'

He smiled now. 'I believe you must be the young lady staying at Castle Grange. Your strange liking for the sea and country has caused some gossip. The villagers are inquisitive when such a charming young lady turns out to be somewhat different from the usual Society girls.'

'Everything about the sea and the beautiful countryside in Devon gives me immense pleasure,' I told him. 'I feel misplaced in the town, for I do not enjoy parties and dancing and the type of life I am expected to live there.'

We had crossed the narrow bridge and to our right

passed a terrace of small cottages, where I was obliged to gather up my skirt as the lane was potholed and muddy. The rain had stopped altogether and from a deep blue sky the sun shone down warm and pleasant again, causing a light steam to rise from the ground as well as from my soaked clothes.

Standing back from the lane and surrounded by clipped green grass stood the most picturesque cottage, newly thatched, I have ever seen.

Charles McClure secured his reins to the saddle and gave his stallion a reassuring pat, leaving him to wander at will, and once more the bulldog came into view from the rear of the cottage.

But now he wasn't growling or barking and looked less ferocious with his short tail wagging its welcome. He didn't even appear to be so large.

'Come and make your apologies to the young lady at once, Humphrey. It's high time you learned the difference between poachers, prowlers and beautiful women.'

I stooped to pat gently the head of the animal, quite handsome in its own way with black, brown and white smooth silky coat.

'But please, Miss Rothesay, it won't do to remain in those clothes a moment longer. You must be soaked to the skin.'

Hesitantly protesting, I followed him to the back of the cottage, clean and neat just as the front appeared. He opened the latched wooden door without knocking, and called as he took care to wipe his boots on the doormat:

'Hannah! I've brought you a visitor.'

The small kitchen was dark, but smelled sweet with a faint aroma of herbs drying. Charles McClure drew me through into the parlour where a woman sat in the window sewing.

As she looked up I was forced to hold my breath as her Madonna-like loveliness captivated me. She was not a raving beauty of Emma's style. Her hair was jet black, sleek and shining as each hair was drawn tightly back to the nape of her neck in a coil. Her face was long and slender to match the hands and fingers which now hastily set aside her work as she greeted Charles McClure with a faint blush enhancing the waxlike cheeks. Her thin lips widened in a tender smile and from the dove-grey eyes she afforded me a warm welcome.

'Hannah, this is Miss Rothesay, Miss Abigail Rothesay I believe you said?'

I nodded in reply to his questioning glance.

'She is staying at Castle Grange with her sister, Mrs. Bond. I'm afraid she was caught in the heavy shower and cannot possibly return in this state.'

Rising from the chair, her dress fell in heavy folds about her trim figure and with graceful charm she held my outstretched hand. The dress, like herself, was plain, but the quality of silk gave it and its wearer distinction.

Charles McClure watched us intently, then looked at me as he introduced her.

'Miss Rothesay, you are welcome, I know, in the home of Hannah Lacey. Edward, her husband, is my agent, and has recently come to live on the estate and help me to manage it. Yes'—he glanced us up and down—'If you'll pardon the presumption, you would appear to my ignorant eyes to be about the same size. Hannah, I'm sure in your wardrobe you can find something for Miss Rothesay to change into?'

Hannah Lacey smiled at him.

'Of course, Mr. Charles, I'll find something.' She led the way to a small door which opened to reveal a twisting staircase.

'Come, Miss Rothesay.'

Charles McClure's eyes followed the gliding movements of Hannah, then with another half-bow toward me as I prepared to follow Hannah, he said:

'I'll send my carriage to take you back to Castle Grange, Miss Rothesay.'

'But really, there's no need,' I protested. 'I walked here, I can return the same way.'

But the elegant Charles McClure shook his head firmly.

'I think not. Your sister might be worried about you. It will be my pleasure to know that you are safely conducted back to Castle Grange.'

With a nod in Hannah's direction he took his leave.

Hannash ushered me into a bedroom at the back of the cottage.

'Do quickly get out of that dress, Miss Rothesay. I am sorry that the weather spoilt your walk. It was an angry shower which surprised us all.'

She left me for a moment while I unbuttoned my dress and let it fall to the floor.

Inquisitively I looked about me at the snow-white hand-crocheted bedspread on the too large bed for the size of the room. My gaze fell on the only other item of furniture, an enormous inlaid mahogany chest which seemed to cry out for lack of space in which to show off its beauty.

This was not the furniture, or even the woman belonging to a humble country cottage. If I felt misplaced in Society life, so much more was Hannah Lacey misplaced in such meagre surroundings, I felt.

She returned, carrying a pale blue walking dress of warm material.

'Try this for size, Miss Rothesay—or you may come to my room and choose for yourself.'

Her voice had an almost sad quality about it.

'Please call me Abbey,' I begged her. 'Everyone does. This dress will do very nicely. I really am sorry to descend upon you like this.'

'I see few people, Abbey. It is a pleasure for me to have company. I shall look forward to further visits when you're out walking this way. This estate has beautiful woods and the garden of the house is delightful. I know Mr. Charles would love you to share its natural beauty. Now, I'll leave you to tidy yourself while I make tea before you leave.'

Later, when I joined her in the parlour, delicate china with a cornflower design graced the white lace cloth upon the small round table, and the home-made scones smelled delicious.

Everything about Hannah Lacey depicted nobility. I knew I was being rude, yet could not refrain from staring at her constantly, and felt a strange emotion reaching out to respond to her gentle charm.

We were going to be friends, of this I was certain.

'How long are you expecting to stay at Castle Grange, Abbey?'

'Until Emma's offspring arrives, and maybe a week or so afterwards, until my sister is up and about again, and the nanny proves suitable.'

'How nice for Mrs. Bond to have a sister to help at a time like this. You are obviously fond of children, Abbey?'

I laughed. 'I must confess, Hannah, I know nothing about them. I feel certain I shall feel much too afraid to handle such a tiny creature with my clumsiness. I'll let you into my guilty secret—I'm really here in disgrace. My parents thought they had found a suitable husband for me, a wealthy, but quite repulsive Earl, and I astonished everyone by having nothing to do with him. Consequently, it was felt desirable to get me out of the way until the scandal dies down.'

Hannah's eyes glistened with amusement.

'How lovely,' she said. 'I do so agree that you should be allowed to choose your own husband. I imagine, though, that to be sent to the country was no punishment to you?'

'Indeed no—quite the contrary. I could stay here for ever.'

'Then we shall have to find a suitor for you in these parts.'

I smiled, and my thoughts darted at once to the handsome man I had just met, Charles McClure. I even felt the warmth of my cheeks increase uneasily—yet, for all I knew, Charles McClure could be and probably was, married.

'I know little of men,' I told Hannah quickly. 'I find Mother Earth much more fascinating, and cannot imagine myself with a home to run and husband to care for.'

'Then enjoy Mother Earth, my dear, for as long as you can. There's time enough to find out the strange ways of men.'

I thought I detected a sudden sharpness of tone, but it was quickly concealed as she rose in answer to Humphrey's growl.

'That will be the carriage. I have enjoyed your visit, Abbey, may it be the first of many.'

'You've been more than kind, Hannah. Yes, I should love to visit you again, indeed it will be necessary to return the dress you have so kindly lent me.'

Hannah walked with me to where the carriage was now waiting after turning on the green. Although I sensed a sadness about the cottage I loved it, and had felt very much at home there.

'Drive slowly through the grounds, Reuben, so that Miss Rothesay can enjoy the view, and get a glimpse of Lyme Towers,' Hannah instructed the driver.

'Indeed, ma'am, I will, though 'tis already falling dusk.'

He was a small, balding man with large white whiskers, and seemed, I thought, a trifle edgy. No doubt he was annoyed at being summoned to take me home and was anxious to be about some task for himself, and far from driving slowly through the grounds, no sooner had we left the narrow lane for a much wider pathway than he set the horses at a brisk gallop.

I did notice the lake we skirted which narrowed, and was spanned with a delightful stonework bridge, and through the trees a building showed up like marble, rising majestically in the gathering dusk, with a pillared balcony covered with trailing evergreens.

Then it was out of my vision and we passed the edge of the woods with fields, and horses in a paddock to the right.

So this was the home of the McClure family of which I had never heard, which was strange, for it depicted great wealth, and from the fleeting glimpse I had had of it I believed to be of more recent and modern architecture.

Quite unlike the rambling wings and turrets of Castle Grange of which I now caught sight, having left the McClure estate and travelled through narrow lanes twisting and turning, a hamlet or farmhouse here and there, and then turning away from the village, leaving the blacksmith's forge on the right, the bakery on the left as we climbed the steep incline which led to the cliff top, and Castle Grange.

With a loud crack of the whip the horses were through the entrance and into the forecourt of my brother-in-law's house.

In the curtaining dusk I could see patches of rain water still standing as the carriage door was opened.

Remembering that I was wearing a borrowed dress,

I hastily gathered the skirt over my arm and prepared to step down steadily, but Reuben held my arm and pulled me down quite roughly.

'Thank you so much for your trouble,' I began, but he had returned to his driver's seat and with a hasty: ' 'Night, miss—no trouble,' hanging on the air, he was away back whence he had come.

Stunned at his rather odd behaviour, I stood and wached, noticing the purple sunset and menacing clouds overhead, when the rattle of the ancient oak door behind me and rustling skirts drew my attention to Emma and Mrs. Thwaites.

'Come inside, Abbey, quickly.' Emma's voice was agitated. 'Where on earth have you been? We've been so worried. Were you caught in the rain? Greville is out on horseback looking for you.'

I realised with dismay that my prolonged absence must have alarmed Emma.

'It's all right, Emma—really. I've come to no harm. The shower was rather heavy and unexpected, and I was obliged to seek shelter, when a charming gentleman named Charles McClure came to my rescue.'

I heard Emma's intake of breath as she clutched at my arm, and with Mrs. Thwaites on the other side I was hustled inside the house.

'Up to your room, Abbey, at once, please,' she begged.

'But why? Really, Emma, I must make allowances for your condition, but please calm yourself.'

'Better do as Mrs. Bond says,' Mrs. Thwaites insisted, guiding me forcibly to the wide staircase.

'Mr. McClure kindly took me to one of his cottages where I met Hannah Lacey and she lent me this dress. She invited me to take tea with her, and then Mr. McClure sent his carriage to bring me home. Wasn't that kind of him, Emma?'

We had reached the first landing now, Emma so beside herself that she hadn't heard a word I had said.

'Mrs. Thwaites,' she commanded. 'Fetch plenty of hot water. Abbey must take a bath at once or she may catch cold.'

'Oh, Emma!' I laughed at such nonsense. 'I am quite all right. It is not the first time I have been out in the rain.'

But protest as I would, the hip bath was brought to my room before the crackling fire, and while Mrs. Thwaites added hot water constantly, I was persuaded to allow my damp-ridden body to benefit from the soaking, to prevent a chill.

Emma chattered quite incoherently the whole time, ordering a hot drink, and the warming pan to be placed in my bed, when suddenly the door was kicked open and Greville Bond stood scowling in the doorway.

'What is the meaning of the McClure carriage being on my land?' he roared.

# *Three*

FOR A SECOND we all gaped open-mouthed at the intrusion. Then Mrs. Thwaites had the presence of mind to pick up the huge towel warming before the fire, and held it in front of me.

Emma began snivelling.

'Greville. Don't be angry. It wasn't Abbey's fault. She got wet and Hannah lent her a dress.'

Still wearing muddy boots Greville Bond took a step nearer, and stretching out his riding crop flicked the towel from Mrs. Thwaites' hands.

'Oh, sir,' she uttered, lowering her eyes with a mixture of shame and fear.

I kept my knees well up, and hugged myself with my arms. From their weakness I took strength and my anger equalled that of Greville Bond.

'Kindly leave my room at once,' I shouted.

'*Your* room! Every stick and stone here belongs to me, Miss Abigail—and don't you forget it. As long as you remain under my roof you will have no dealings with any McClure, or Lacey come to that.'

Gradually as his leering eyes feasted upon my nakedness his tone softened.

I became all too aware of my predicament, having seldom given much thought to my body or clothes in the past.

My eyes blazed fiercely.

'Get out of my room, sir, immediately, or I shall throw the bath water at you,' I shrieked.

Greville's eyes narrowed as with half a grin he spoke viciously.

'I'm tempted to allow you to try, Miss Abigail,' then with a loathsome shout of laughter he left the room banging the door behind him.

Mrs. Thwaites hastily caught up a jug and began pouring water over me again.

'Stop it! Stop it at once,' I begged her. 'That water is cold—and kindly do me the honour of leaving me to finish bathing and dressing alone. In future my door stays locked. Now I can understand the reason for your unwelcome attentions. I shall look forward to hearing just why the McClure family are unmentionable, Emma.'

Emma was still sniffing.

'I don't know, Abbey——just some silly old feud or other.'

I was truly grateful for their departure, but obliged to laugh at myself as I brushed my unruly hair before the mirror later.

My love of Mother Nature had brought me down to earth with a bump. Little had I ever thought to find myself in such a situation—and certainly not with my own brother-in-law.

How, I wondered, could Emma enjoy Greville's crude manners, let alone being the wife of such a man? I shuddered at the thought.

Why couldn't she have chosen a man like Charles McClure? Equally masculine, equally fearless, but with a kinder nature, especially where women were concerned. But I doubted that he was Emma's type. She had made her choice, foolish though it appeared to me, and was expecting Greville's child. Her pretty feminine ways obviously appealed to Greville, she was but a piece of potter's clay in his hands, yielding to his every whim, while it seemed my less feeble nature only served to arouse his coarseness. Oh, well, the weeks would soon pass by and I should be thinking of returning to my parents.

I sat sipping the hot drink Mrs. Thwaites had sent up for me, watching the red ashes turn to white powder as the last of the logs burnt away.

Much as I disliked Greville Bond I was happy with Emma, in her home, and quickly put aside all thoughts of having to leave Castle Grange.

The next day I woke to a still atmosphere. Looking out of the window I saw that everywhere was shrouded in a gloomy mist. There would be no walks for me today, and perhaps just as well.

I sat for a while with Emma, but she seemed preoccupied, and Greville was absent from the house all day.

Mrs. Thwaites drew the curtains early after tea, shutting out the depressing dampness while Emma and I sat round the fire.

'Emma,' I said, attempting to break the icy tension between us. 'I'm sorry if I caused some distress yesterday. How could I have possibly known that Greville was at loggerheads with the McClure family?'

Emma managed a wan smile as the firelight danced across her pale face. Her eyes, usually laughing, seemed vacant as she stared at me and sighed.

'You couldn't have known, Abbey. Indeed, I know nohing of the McClure family myself. Greville is quite adamant about having no dealings with them and refuses even to discuss the matter. Now I have a headache. I think I shall go to bed.' She rose awkwardly, as if the unborn infant within her was, at this moment, a great burden to her.

'Are you all right, Emma? Shall I come and help you?'

She waved me aside. 'No, Abbey—Mrs. Thwaites will already be upstairs, I expect.'

The house became very still after she had left. I had no desire to go to bed yet, it was still early evening, so this was my chance to visit the library.

From the lamp I lit one of the spare candles, and went across the hall to the door on the left of the front door.

There was no fire in the oak-panelled room and it smelled musty, even though a small room leading off was constantly used by Greville as his office.

Holding the tall brass candlestick high, I scanned the shelves for books of local history. In one corner a cupboard with glass doors was securely locked, but I could see that it housed nothing but volumes of poetry.

I had the impression that I must be the first visitor to the library for some considerable time, apart from the servants who cleaned there. Novels, autobiographies, maps, as well as hymn and prayer books, were there in abundance, but not a history book could I find anywhere. My disappointment made me somewhat despondent as I realised I must give up the fruitless search, when a sudden howling wind, seeming to come from the other smaller room, made me shiver with cold.

The candle flickered and went out.

Fortunately, I had not closed the library door, so that a small amount of light was gained from the hall candelabra.

In the doorway leading to Greville's room I saw again the shadow of a monk!

I clutched the bodice of my gown, very much afraid when a loud thud at my feet startled me.

Anxiously I looked down, but in the darkness could see nothing. When I glanced towards the doorway again the shadow had disappeared.

Eventually I summoned sufficient courage to return to the hall quickly, and relight my candle.

Hesitantly I crept back to Greville's room, but there was no one there.

This old house must be making me fanciful, I told myself angrily, and as I went back into the library I kicked something. It was a book—small, leather-bound, almost new in appearance, even though a light film of dust shaded its title: *The Receding Coast of Devon.*

I held the candle higher and looked up, but could see no other books about to descend upon me from the ceiling, nor indeed any place from where this one had fallen. But I was too intrigued to linger in this cold place and silently hurried upstairs to my room.

Throwing another log on the fire, I settled myself in a large armchair to read.

The first page or two told of crumbling buildings and falling cliffs all along the south coast of Devon, with many a cave, only accessible by boat, left for the benefit of smugglers.

The room grew warm and I sensed a comforting presence compelling me to turn the pages quickly instead of reading the book, which had been written in the late eighteenth century, from cover to cover.

I flicked through to nearer the middle pages when I glimpsed the name of Castle Rock.

'The name does not come from any early Castles in the area, but from the two rocky headlands, at a distance silhouetted against the sky appearing like Castles. Between them in the valley stands the ruins of an old monastery believed to have been partially destroyed by a freak storm raging in from the sea in about 1703, killing all the inhabitants who were at supper. Shortly afterwards the agent's offices in

Exeter were gutted by fire, thus losing all documents as to its inheritance.

'The two dominating Devon families of Castle Rock, the McClures and the Bonds, have both over the years laid claim to the ruins and surrounding land, but without confirmation.

'Rumour has it that the Monastery was formerly a large house owned by a woman named Agnes Drummond, whose only son, Francis Drummond, when in his early teens announced that he was to become a Monk.

'The woman, distressed at her son's decision, committed suicide. Her existence is confirmed by a gravestone bearing her name, and the year of her death, 1685, in the churchyard of the Parish Church in Castle Rock. Who she was and whether there are any relatives is not known, but many conflicting rumours circulate throughout that part of Devon.'

I read this over again. So, there had once been a monk in these parts, indeed many monks. But what was that to me? And why should any of them seek to visit me?

Long after I had taken to my bed my mind remained stimulated concerning events of the past, and indeed to more recent happenings, such as the pleasure I had experienced in meeting Charles McClure, as well as the shame of the subsequent occurrence.

At least now I understood to some extent that the feud beween the two families was most likely caused by this no-man's-land laying idle in the valley. Yet both men surely had sufficient acreage with which to be prosperous, and should have been satisfied.

Being Sunday, breakfast next morning was later than usual. Greville joined Emma and me almost as soon as we had taken our places. He looked suitably attired for the Sabbath and seemed reasonably pleasant.

'Shall you go to church this morning, Emma my dear?' he asked. 'It is bleak out and no mistake.'

'Yes, we can all go together in the carriage. I'm sure even Abbey would not wish to walk today.'

I met Greville's smile with some embarrassment.

'Suitably dressed I shouldn't mind one bit,' I told my sister. 'But the ride will be enjoyable for us both.'

'Yes, you're right. I can do with the outing, it doesn't do to sit about at home.'

Greville sat with his coachman, Sam, while Emma and I enjoyed passing through the grounds and the village. I had intended to speak to Emma of the book I had found, but decided against it for some reason which I could not fathom.

It was not raining, but dull, and we passed many of the estate workers and their families, who jumped out of the way as the carriage approached, for fear of getting their Sunday clothes mud-splashed.

At the foot of the hill we reached the crossroads where the Castle Inn was situated, and as we turned to take the main Exeter road towards the little church, another carriage came at us from the opposite direction.

The driver managed to pull in the reins, but the horses were travelling too fast and had difficulty in avoiding us. As I was sitting on that side of our carriage I noticed that the driver of the other carriage was Reuben, from the McClure estate, who with a great shout succeeded in turning the horses and carriage at the last moment, thus avoiding a nasty collision.

Greville was no doubt feeling pleased that he had delayed the McClure carriage and we could hear him laughing with Sam.

The church was set back from the main road in an isolated basin of greenery, its bells, pealing out the call to worship, echoing in the surrounding hills. As we stepped in through the lych-gate the strains of organ music reached us.

The rear pews were filled with villagers and many children, and Greville led the way to the Bond pew at the front, on the left side of the aisle, allowing Emma and me to sit first.

During the singing of the first hymn I became aware of some disturbance behind us. The singing sounded less avid, the parson took out a large white handkerchief, and appeared to be at safe disadvantage.

It was then I followed Emma's gaze and saw Charles McClure taking his place on the opposite side of the aisle to Greville.

As the service proceeded it was clear that the parson was labouring under some strain, though I could see no reason for it. True, Charles McClure had not attended a Sunday service during my stay at Castle Grange, and it was usual for the gentry to attend, but I presumed he had been engaged on some business outside the village perhaps.

Although I had read of the feud between the two landowners, I had given little thought to the severity of the matter until now, as I glanced along at Greville's large hands resting on his knees, fists clenched and knuckles white. Emma too seemed unable to concenrate during the sermon and constantly fidgeted.

After the service had ended, Greville was the first to leave his seat, and once more we stood outside as people exchanged light conversation, and Emma's friends anxiously enquired after her health.

Curious as to which direction the gravestone of Agnes Drummond was, I began to wander on alone, when heavy footsteps vibrated behind me.

I turned to find Charles McClure at my side.

'Good morning, Miss Rothesay. I trust you're none the worse for your outing the other day?'

'Thank you for your concern, Mr. McClure, I'm very well, and grateful for your kindness.'

It was not often that I blushed and now I could not tell whether my cheeks rapidly grew crimson because of Charles McClure's attention or because I felt guilty knowing that Greville was somewhere, I was convinced, about to fly into a rage.

'I'm afraid the change in the weather is preventing you from enjoying the open air. I hope it will soon favour you again.'

At that moment Emma called me.

'Come, Abbey, we must go.'

Charles McClure bowed towards Emma.

'Good day, ma'am,' he said pleasantly.

Emma's cold stare and brief acknowledgement astounded me and I felt somewhat degraded.

'I'm delighted to make your acquaintance, Mrs. Bond, and am truly sorry that Lyme Towers has no lady, so that we could be honoured to invite you to take tea at the house.'

'I quite understand, sir,' Emma managed politely, and taking my arm guided me to the carriage where Greville was waiting.

As he helped me into the carriage he whispered:

'I've given you a warning, Miss Abigail, but if it's a fight you want . . . ?'

I refrained from retorting and watched with interest from the carriage window, as Charles McClure greeted Hannah Lacey, whom I had not noticed inside the church. Taking her arm, he led her towards his waiting carriage. I felt grieved that I had not had the opportunity of speaking with her, but almost at once we set off for Castle Grange.

The next few days confined my activities to the house and Emma's company. She frequently complained now of her condition and looked forward to getting the confinement over and done with, so that she could wear her pretty gowns again and take her place in Society.

The mist hung lifeless for days, enveloping Castle Grange in a melancholy cloud, but at last I woke one morning to find the sun shining almost too brilliantly for a late October day.

Looking out of my window, the sea glistened and the seagulls cried out their invitation to join them at play.

Even Emma appeared in better spirits at breakfast.

'Greville is taking me to Exeter today, Abbey, there are still a few necessities for the baby. Greville has business with the bank there, so we shall make a day of it, as I may not feel like going that far again for some time. Would you like to come?'

'Oh, Emma, would you think me rude if I declined? I'd much rather walk in these parts on such a lovely day.'

'Please yourself, of course, my dear Abbey. But don't go too far and get lost. Remember the mist may come up again quite rapidly.'

'I shall take care, Emma. You go off and enjoy yourself with Greville. I may even go across the meadows towards the village, and purchase my few requisites there.'

But reaching the village was not the simple walk I had anticipated.

I walked across the meadows where the sheep and cows grazed, coming to a wood where the soft coo of the wood pigeon made a refreshing change from the constant cry of the seagulls. I believed the wood extended to the edge of Greville's estate, with the village beyond.

The bracken and leaves smelled earthy, and as I ran down the sloping pathway I heard a dog bark in the distance.

At that moment I came to a stream, quite wide and fast-flowing. Wondering in which direction I should find a suitable place to cross, I heard the echo of a horn through the trees, followed by the excited chatter of the hounds in full cry.

Within minutes I was surrounded by persistent hounds, sniffing round my skirts, and horses jumping the stream.

Shielding my eyes from the spray, I looked through my fingers and met the teasing smile of Charles McClure.

## *Four*

CHARLES MCCLURE shouted orders to another horseman, and I was indeed relieved to see them all go off at great speed, the shrill voice of the hunting horn getting fainter as they vanished beyond the woods.

But Charles McClure remained, jumping down from his horse with a gay laugh.

'My dear Miss Rothesay, it seems imperative that our paths should cross, but I am sorry that you were not invited to the hunt. You do ride, I am sure?'

'Yes—oh, yes, Mr. McClure—but I think my brother-in-law would be displeased if I joined in your sport.'

Charles McClure arched his eyebrows in agreement.

'Yes, I fear you're right.' He pursed his lips thoughtfully. 'So you are taking the opportunity of walking on this fine day?'

'I was under the impression that I was still on Greville's land.' I hastened to excuse my presence in the wood.

'Oh, you are, Miss Rothesay, you are. The hunt chases the fox regardless of whose land it is, though we do obtain the local farmers' permission to hunt on their land, and they are only too anxious to see the foxes kept down. I trust that you were not too alarmed?'

I smiled, remembering that this was not the first time he had come to my rescue.

'It seems evident that I am bound to become accustomed to such incidents,' I said. 'I only hope the country animals will accept me as part of the landscape eventually.'

He threw back his head and laughed, his deep, rich voice echoing through the trees, as if they all joined in his merrymaking.

'I am sure the animals and birds are as pleased as I to encounter such a charming lady among nature's most beautiful countryside.'

That he was teasing I felt certain, but I lowered my gaze and found to my discomfort that another beautiful creature had sprung to mind—Hannah Lacey.

No wonder she looked at him with such tenderness, for he was indeed a flatterer, and I fancied that he would pay her much the same attention.

'May I offer you a ride on Duke to your destination?'

'Thank you, no. I was, I hoped, taking the right direction towards the village. I have delayed you in your sport, please continue on your way.'

'That is of no consequence now. They will be some distance away and I should have difficulty in catching them. May I walk with you, Miss Rothesay?'

I could think of nothing I should enjoy more at that moment, yet I felt shy and uneasy in his company, no doubt paying some heeds to Greville's warning.

'I think I must turn back. There appears to be no way to cross the stream.'

'Allow me to show you. Some distance downstream it narrows and there are stones in shallower water to enable you to cross.'

We walked side by side, in silence at first, taking care where we placed our feet to avoid the muddy patches, and it was necessary for me to lift my skirt a little, though I took care not to reveal more than my ankle.

Duke, the black stallion, paused every now and

then, cocking one ear and listening, then whinnying and pawing the ground with one hoof.

Charles McClure patted him reassuringly.

'It's all right, Duke, old boy. There will be other times to join in the hunt.'

'Your horse evidently approves of the sport, Mr. McClure?'

Charles McClure laughed. 'This is his first experience. I felt it was time Lyme Towers revived the sport of my forefathers.'

'So this is a new venture for the farmers of Castle Rock?' I asked, somewhat surprised.

'Yes, indeed. I'm afraid the McClure estate has been neglected for some years now. My father, old and ill, lived alone, apart from his few servants and labourers, who simply took care of the necessities. When he died a year ago I had thought to dispose of the property, as I have not lived in these parts in recent years. But coming back—like you,'—he smiled down at me—'I find I too cannot bear to part with it, and have decided to take my place at Lyme Towers, and feel it my duty to keep the McClure name in evidence in the locality and I hope to open up a more socially congenial atmosphere among the inhabitants. There is a great deal of work to be done, but we must also have our fun, so the hunt is only the beginning. In ten days' time there will be the hunt ball to be held at Lyme Towers. I shall, of course, be sending formal invitation to Castle Grange.'

'That sounds quite splendid,' I said. 'Only . . .'

'Only . . . ? Your brother-in-law will not allow you to attend?'

I glanced across at him, wondering whether I should speak of the century-old feud over useless land, but decided against it.

'Come, Miss Rothesay, I'm sure you can persuade

him to escort both his lovely wife and your good self to enjoy a social occasion?'

'Greville does not seem inclined towards a social life at all,' I said. 'He does not seem the type to accept such invitations, but perhaps I am wrong.'

Charles McClure stopped, pointing to a double row of flat stones placed across the stream.

'See, there is but little water here, allow me to help you.'

The stream was narrow now and in a second or two I was standing on the other side.

From among the dense growth of trees I could hear woodcutters at work, as I followed my companion along a cart-track. Then just as suddenly we were out in the sunlight again and bordering a green field.

'Beyond those cottages, Miss Rothesay, is the village, so I'll bid you good day, if you're certain you wish to continue on foot.'

'Thank you for showing me the way, Mr. McClure. When I have completed my business in the village I shall return by the road to Castle Grange.'

He raised his hat before mounting the handsome Duke once more, and, with a charming smile in my direction, set off across the field at a gallop.

As I continued on my way I wondered about Charles McClure. Although the heir to Lyme Towers, it would seem he was something of a stranger in these parts, so what could Greville Bond have against him? Why such hatred?

But I did not worry unduly about these affairs which, after all, were no concern of mine. Probably I would never know, for if Greville refused to discuss it even with Emma he would surely not divulge such private matters to me, and Charles McClure—well, Charles McClure seemed to be less vindictive, I felt, and if he was to send an invitation to the ball to

Castle Grange, might it not mean he was offering an olive branch?

But, alas, when I sat at luncheon a few days later with Emma, Greville came in seething with rage. He became very red in the face and could only splutter oaths.

'Dearest,' Emma remonstrated, trying to pacify her outraged husband. 'Whatever can the matter be?'

At first he ignored her, then glancing round he caught sight of me. Now I could see the plain envelope and the two halves of a broken seal, from which he had taken a white card with fine gold lettering.

It must be the invitation.

*'You . . .'* he roared in my direction. *'You* must be responsible for this.'

'Responsible for what?' I asked innocently.

'Charles McClure has had the audacity to send *us* an invitation to his hunt ball,' he said, waving the card in my face.

'Why should I be responsible, pray? Surely it is a very kind gesture on his part?'

'Don't meddle, Abbey. Don't interfere in things about which you know nothing. I have told you before—and I'll tell you once more—we'll have no dealings now, or ever, with the McClure family.'

'May I ask why, Greville?' I ventured, while Emma frowned and put her fingers to her lips in great agitation as she shook her head quite crossly at me. 'I'm surprised at a man of your position being so openly against another family in the same district. It can't be a good example to the locals.'

'I'll thank you not to preach to me, miss . . .'

'You must realise, Abbey,' Emma broke in, 'in my condition, with only a month to go, we could hardly accept such an invitation.'

'Then kindly accept on my behalf,' I said, shortly.

'Certainly not!' Greville said, angrily.

'Really, Abbey—you must be obsessed,' Emma said. 'You know you cannot go without an escort.'

'Then I must find one, mustn't I? I shall seek Hannah Lacey's help. She and her husband will surely be going, they shall be my chaperones.'

'Abbey, I forbid it—do you hear? Absolutely forbid it!' and Greville Bond banged his fist on the dining table before striding from the room, tossing the invitation into the fire as he went.

'Now look what you've done, Abbey! How could you? Grev's had nothing to eat, and now he'll sulk, and like as not take his ill temper out on the farm workers.'

'As long as he doesn't take it out on you, Emma. Anyway, he'll soon get over it. I'm sorry, but I refuse to be party to such a silly disagreement.'

'Have you seen Charles McClure again, Abbey?'

'Yes, as a matter of fact I have. When you went off to Exeter the other day I met the hunt in the woods. Mr. McClure stopped and spoke to me. He mentioned the ball and seemed to be seriously offering an olive branch, Emma. I think Greville is making a big mistake in not accepting.'

'And I think you're making a mistake in interfering. Anyway, the invitation is burnt now, so you can forget we ever received one.'

'It may not be dispensed with quite so easily, Emma. Should I meet Mr. McClure, and he mentions it, I shall certainly let him know *my* feelings on the matter.'

'You *are* obsessed with the man!' Emma cried. 'Abbey, you cannot be serious. While you are living under Greville's roof you must honour his wishes. Remember, it is good of him to have you here.'

'Then I'll pack my things and take a room at the inn. I want no favours from you or Greville. I thought you wanted company and indeed some help when your child arrives?'

'Oh, Abbey, don't let's quarrel,' Emma whined. 'But you are making things very difficult for me. Try not to upset Greville so much. Of course we want you to stay.'

'You may, Emma, but Greville makes it quite clear that I have outstayed my welcome.'

'Well, I won't hear of such a thing. I shall need someone of my own family when the time comes. It's a great pity that Charles McClure ever came back.'

'Back from where?' I asked.

'The Army. He's had a very successful career in the Army, so Mrs. Thwaites tells me, and was thinking of selling up in these parts. Evidently he has changed his mind.'

'Surely that is quite understandable? He wishes to carry on the family tradition, and put the McClure name back among social propriety.'

Emma sighed. 'Then, no doubt he'll be looking for a wife.'

'Perhaps he already has one. If he's been away for sometime, who's to say he hasn't a wife ready to take her place at Lyme Towers?'

'No, Abbey, he has no wife, of that I'm sure. No doubt his way of life in the Army is somewhat different to that to whch we are accustomed. I suspect he's something of a philanderer, especially where women are concerned.'

'It seems quite disgusting to me to blacken a man's character when you don't really know him, Emma.'

Emma's dark eyes searched mine, causing my cheeks to grow crimson. I was not certain of my feelings. Never before had any man been of the slightest interest to me, let alone causing me embarrassment as the name of Charles McClure did. Obviously I was flattered by his charm, as well as feeling some sympathy for this black sheep, so despised by Greville Bond.

As October's days grew short, the weather became changeable, frequently alternating between bitterly cold days with torrential rainy ones and then for no apparent reason a mild, sunny day with blue skies would dawn, to heighten our pleasure and fit us for the coming winter months.

It was on such a morning as this that Emma decided we should walk to the village. She had not been well with a severe head cold, as well as the increased weight adding discomfort, but overnight it was as if she had been rejuvenated and was bouncing with energy.

Mrs. Thwaites voiced her concern at Emma's proposed journey, but I assured her we would walk very slowly, and Emma agreed to have the carriage meet us by the inn some two hours later.

On my last visit to the village I had purchased a cane basket as a gift to Emma, who now wished to purchase the muslin with which to cover it. I had purposely left the choice to my sister, having little knowledge of such delicate fineries myself.

The little drapery shop with its bow-fronted windows was run by two middle-aged sisters, the Misses Fanny and Hetty Bell. As we walked up the steps the shop door opened and Hannah Lacey stood in the doorway accompaned by Charles McClure.

Hannah was wearing the same simple dress in which I had first seen her, of soft turquoise blue, with a matching bonnet adorned only with feathers, and draped about her shoulder hung a large shawl, bordered with deep lace.

Charles McClure clicked his heels and bowed gracefully, his knee-length cape with turned-down collar opening to reveal the immaculate waist-fitted, double-breasted tail-coat and slim trousers. He kept his Cumberland hat in his hand with cane and gloves, as he held the door open for us.

'Good day, ladies, what a pleasure,' he said. 'I trust you are both well?'

Emma's cheeks were quite flushed as she replied, and would have hurried on into the shop, but Charles McClure detained her.

'I do hope we are to have the pleasure of your company at Lyme Towers for the ball, Mrs. Bond?'

Emma eyed him demurely.

'I'm afraid not, I could hardly . . .' she began, when he cut her short.

'But we should love to have you, even if you cannot join in, you would enjoy watching the others dancing.'

'It was good of you to invite us, Mr. McClure, but my husband would wish me to decline on behalf of us all,' Emma told him firmly.

'I cannot believe Miss Rothesay feels the same?' He looked over Emma's head at me, standing on a lower step behind Emma.

I knew that I wanted to go to the ball more than anything else in the world.

'It would give me great pleasure to accept your invitation,' I said, 'but, alas, I have no chaperone.'

It was then that Hannah Lacey interjected, as she touched Emma lightly on the arm.

'Indeed, Mrs. Bond, I am truly sorry that you feel you cannot attend such a lively function, but I'm sure you would not wish your sister to be left out. It will be our pleasure to fetch and escort her—you would like that, Abbey?'

'Thank you, Hannah, I shall look forward to it,' I said, meeting the dove-grey eyes with gratitude.

'Well, er, um, I'm sure I don't know,' Emma stammered.

'Have no fear, Mrs. Bond,' Charles McClure said, looking down at Emma kindly. 'Miss Rothesay will be well looked after, and is, after all, of an age when she can surely make her own decision?'

'You're most kind,' Emma said, softly, and pushed past him into the shop, where the two little proprietors stood behind their display of cottons and lace, watching the proceedings wide-eyed, their beaky noses quick to sniff out a scandal to relate to their inquisitive clientele.

As the day of the ball drew near my excitement diminished, as I experienced some degree of shame.

Lucy, a young girl from the village who was to become the nursemaid when Emma's baby arrived, took up residence at Castle Grange, which indicated that Emma's time was short, and my place was at home with her.

But Emma was excited now at my visiting Lyme Towers, even though she had not mentioned it to Greville, and had expressed the hope that he would be away from the house on the evening of the ball as indeed he frequently was. Only Mrs. Thwaites shared our secret as we prepared my gown of golden silk, which was cut very low off the shoulders, with a deep falling lace collar of two layers.

The wide skirt was to be supported by several petticoats, and the sleeves were of the popular mameluke design, full, but tied in puffs at intervals from shoulder to wrist.

Emma's reflection in the mirror as she dressed my hair in ringlets a good hour before the carriage was due to arrive looked pale and frightened.

'Emma, shall I not go, after all?' I blurted out. 'I ought not to have been so selfish. My place is here with you.'

'Abbey, calm yourself,' Emma laughed. 'You know

you *must* go, now that the Laceys are to come for you. I'm feeling fine, and Mrs. Thwaites is here if I need her. You are so lucky, how I envy you, Abbey, my dear. To be dressing up and going to a ball, and at Lyme Towers of all places. Do store it all up in your mind, Abbey, so that you can tell me all about it afterwards. Charles McClure will be the perfect host, of that I am sure.'

Although I felt full of remorse, I too felt apprehensive at the sight of Lyme Towers, which was aglow with light as our carriage drew up at the decorative stone steps, where a footman opened the carriage door and led us up to the balcony, and then to the ballroom beyond.

Such was my tension that I had scarcely noticed Hannah's husband, Edward, beyond our brief introduction in the carriage.

Now, after being announced and greeted warmly by our host, I observed Edward Lacey with startled interest.

He was of medium height, broad, and, like our host, elegantly dressed with a waistcoat of velvet, while Charles McClure looked distinguished in black and gold brocade over his finely pleated evening shirt and white bow-tie. In contrast to his tanned skin and dark hair, Edward Lacey was noticeable with his round, rosy-cheeked face framed with bright carroty hair and side-whiskers.

His manner was gay, almost flippant, and I frequently caught a remonstrating look from Hannah, who as always wore the simplest of dresses, in a rich blue taffeta, the pleated bodice having a round lace-edged neckline.

My dance card was quickly filled, and to my delight I found I was the honoured guest to be escorted to supper by Charles McClure, and afterwards it seemed was to be his dancing partner for the rest of the evening.

Everything surpassed my wildest dreams, and as I danced I was greatly impressed by the décor of the large ballroom, with walls of palest green tapestries, which like the numerous large mirrors were gilt edged with a leaf design. From the fine filigree stucco ceiling hung magnificent crystal chandeliers which seemed to sway to rhythm to the music and the vibration of the many people enjoying the ball.

Nor did it escape my notice that Edward Lacey danced only the first cotillion with his wife, after which he seemed to find a variety of fashionable young ladies with whom to amuse himself, while Hannah frequently became Charles McClure's partner, a situation which constantly puzzled me and which I failed to comprehend.

At last supper was announced and Charles McClure held out his arm to me.

'I trust you are enjoying yourself, Miss Rothesay?' he asked, as with envying eyes upon us he led the way across the vast ballroom to the huge, richly carved doors.

'Indeed I am, Mr. McClure, a truly joyous occasion for me,' I replied, at the same time remembering vaguely Emma, who was sitting alone at Castle Grange probably starting at every sound lest Greville should return and discover my absence.

But my thoughts were not allowed to dwell on such unpleasant suppositions.

'You look quite charming tonight, Miss Rothesay, if I may be permitted to be personal. This is rather a change, is it not, from our usual rendezvous, when you suddenly appear before me as a country maiden, bonnet ribbons blowing in the wind and skirts gathered up for protection. I seem to remember you telling me you do not care for parties?'

'There can always be an exception, I hope, Mr. McClure?'

'I think we have known one another sufficiently long to drop the formalities now, Miss Rothesay. I should be obliged if you would call me Charles.'

'Thank you,' I said, at a loss for words. 'My name is Abigail, but everyone calls me Abbey.'

'Then I shall be honoured to do the same. Abbey . . . Abbey,' he repeated softly, like a connoisseur of wine savouring the flavour. 'Yes, my dear, it suits you. One is apt to associate nuns and monks with an Abbey, and they are of the highest order, as well as being hard-working folk. I think I am right in supposing that you like to be busy rather than idling the hours away?'

'I will admit to preferring having something to do. I am very fond of reading, but there any similarity with a nun must end, I fear.'

Charles looked down at me and smiled, and as we enjoyed the lavish supper and the dancing which lasted until one in the morning, my ecstasy was unsurmountable.

That I had actually enjoyed such an evening was unbelievable and that Charles McClure's lips upon my hand could arouse such excitement, which lingered even as we drew up at the door of Castle Grange, made me feel quite guilty.

After whispering good night to Hannah and Edward Lacey, I tiptoed towards the forbidding door.

The handle responded to my touch easily, and in an instant I was inside.

A single candle was burning low on the hall table, left for my benefit by the considerate Mrs. Thwaites, no doubt.

I lifted my skirts and petticoats in order to creep up the stairs, when in the half-light my gaze rested upon a pair of large boots upon the first step.

Slowly, the candle flickering in my trembling hand, I allowed my gaze to travel upwards, to meet the angry expression of Greville Bond.

## *Five*

AS WE FACED EACH OTHER, hostile, silent, from somewhere above came a great shriek.

Wild thoughts racked my whirling brain as I gasped, wondering what he could possibly have done to Emma.

Then another sound echoed through the silence, at first only a whimper, followed by louder cries.

'No . . . no . . . it can't be. The baby isn't due for two more weeks,' I said, moving round Greville to get to Emma.

But he barred my way.

'A fine sister you turned out to be, Miss Abigail,' he sneered. 'You will go to your room. You shall *not* see Emma or the child tonight!'

He turned and mounted the stairs two at a time.

I followed lamely, utterly dejected.

Before going along to my room, I paused at the head of the stairs, looking anxiously towards Emma's door, hoping for a sight of Mrs. Thwaites, or even Lucy—anyone who might give me news of my sister —but the house was desolate in its stillness.

No voices could be heard through the thick oak doors and no further cries—was the baby all right?

I forced myself to go into my room where a small fire still burned in the hearth.

After pacing the room for what seemed like hours, I eventually discarded my clothes and prepared for bed.

But just as I was folding back the covers a creak

outside on the landing made me stop and listen. I heard the unmistakable sound of someone going downstairs, so I opened my door and through the crack saw Greville, still in his working clothes, disappearing from view.

I waited and listened, knowing that he would be doing the same, expecting me to grasp the opportunity to see my sister. But no one stirred, so I closed my door gently and went to bed, tossing, turning and listening, drowsy, yet unable to sleep because of the misery I felt at leaving Emma.

Suddenly I blinked!

A shaft of light passed across the ceiling. I was aware of someone near, someone's laboured breathing.

'Miss Abigail? You awake, Miss Abigail?'

Was it my ghost taunting me again?

But in an instant I was sitting up as I recognised the ample form of Mrs. Thwaites.

'What is it, Mrs. Thwaites?' I whispered back. 'Is Emma all right—and the baby?'

'Come, the master be drinking his-self silly downstairs—Mrs. Bond wants you.'

Quickly I threw a large shawl round my shoulders and followed Mrs. Thwaites to the east wing and Emma's room.

She lay motionless in the big bed, her golden hair lifeless around her weary face on the pillow.

'Emma, Emma!' I cried, as I kissed her forehead. 'Can you ever forgive me—had you no notion that the baby had started before I went out?'

She clung to me and I felt the salty moisture of her tears on my face.

'Emma, are you all right? It's all over now, and the baby—he is . . . ?'

'It's a girl.' She spat the words out spitefully.

'But that's lovely,' I told her, as I cradled her in my

arms. 'As long as she's healthy what does it matter?'

'Greville won't even look at her,' she sobbed.

'He will, Emma, he will. Give him time, he won't be able to resist his daughter, and he'll soon realise that there's always a next time.'

Emma turned away from me and cried bitterly.

'It was awful, Abbey, awful! I never want to go through that again, and the baby's so tiny. I'm glad you weren't here—glad. Oh, Abbey, if only I could change places with you. Do tell me about the ball. What's Lyme Towers like?'

'Tomorrow, Emma, there's plenty of time for me to tell you about that tomorrow. Now you must rest, please be quiet and try to sleep.'

I smoothed the sheets, and then crept to the cradle where a tiny red-faced bundle slept.

'She's lovely, Emma—quite lovely.'

Emma managed to smile through wet lashes and I tiptoed back to the landing where Mrs. Thwaites was keeping guard.

'My sister is all right, isn't she, Mrs. Thwaites?' I asked.

'Yes, Miss Abigail——frightened, she were—it came too sudden like, you see, good thing t'were only a little 'un. Five and half pounds, miss, but a little darlin', all the same. I'll see she does all right—and tht baby too. Ssh! I can hear 'im moving about, you best get back to your room, miss, mustn't let 'im know as how I let you in to see your sister. Don't you worry, she'll be as right as ninepence after a good night's sleep.'

In the darkness I lay thinking about Emma. Poor Emma, who tried so hard to please Greville, but for whom I could see no future happiness with such a man.

If she was really happy why the interest in Lyme

Towers? I suspected that she, like Hannah Lacey, was over-awed by Charles McClure's charm. Strange that both these women had such seemingly unsuitable husbands, I thought, for Edward Lacey too appeared to me to have absolutely nothing in common with the genteel Hannah.

Perhaps that was how marriages were. Mine certainly would have been had I married the Earl—and had I married the Earl I wouldn't be here now, so that my meeting Charles McClure couldn't have happened.

I turned over and closed my eyes, contented with the memory of my evening in his company. But married, even to him, who knows what turn of character he might show. . . .

As I dressed next morning, not much later than usual despite the shortness of the night, I thought happily of my new status: 'Aunt Abbey'. I had a niece and I intended to spoil her to make up for her father's lack of interest.

I dreaded a meeting with Greville, but thankfully there was no sign of him as I breakfasted alone.

Maud saw to my needs in an uncommunicative way, and just as I was finishing Mrs. Thwaites came into the breakfast room.

'Good morning, Mrs. Thwaites. How is Emma this morning?'

'Tired, but a little more colour in her cheeks, and she's managed a little gruel.'

'I am so sorry I was not here at a time when I must have been needed. Was Greville very angry when he discovered my absence?'

Mrs. Thwaites gave an impatient grunt.

'He wasn't in himself above a few minutes, miss, when you arrived.'

'Really? Poor Emma, it must have seemed as if we'd all deserted her. So if I had been home just ten minutes earlier he would never have known?

Mrs. Thwaites nodded.

'But where was he, Mrs. Thwaites? Does he often stay out until the early hours?'

'Frequently, miss.' She laughed. 'But then—well, it's easy to see you and your sister don't come from these parts. There's plenty for a man to do around here come darkness.'

I looked at the housekeeper in astonishment.

'What do you mean?' I demanded. 'Are you suggesting Mr. Bond is about some evil business at night?'

'Like as not, miss. 'Tis up to every man to make a bit for his-self like, on the side.'

'I don't understand you, Mrs. Thwaites?'

'Come now, Miss Abigail. I don't have to tell you about the smuggling that goes on all along the coast from Cornwall, as far as Dorset, surely?'

'Smuggling?' I echoed, stupidly.

'Everyone does it, miss. Even my dear departed Tom done his share. Not that he ever went so far as to entice the ships on to the rocks, mind you . . .'

I must have gaped open-mouthed at Mrs. Thwaites.

'You—you mean they actually—help—to cause a ship to get smashed to pieces on the rocks?' I stammered.

' 'Tis thought so. There's the regular French vessels—and some Spanish that calls in close by with brandy and wines, but then there's many on a stormy night what gets shipwrecked. Customs man gets suspicious but can't catch no one. One of them officers got killed—fell over the cliff he did.'

'How awful,' I said, visualising the horror of such a fate, while Mrs. Thwaites cleared her throat and set about her work, obviously a little guilty at having revealed too much.

So now I knew what kept Greville Bond about at such strange hours, but where were these rocks? The shingle beach below Castle Grange and westwards was too open. Then I remembered my walk up on the headland, and the hidden building below—ruins of the old monastery I had learned from the book. No doubt the sea had seeped its way in at that point, making an excellent cover for would-be smugglers.

Try as I would, even with caring for Emma and the baby, I could not dispense with the curiosity aroused. I longed for a morning free to walk and explore, but my duties to my sister demanded most of my time during the next three weeks.

Emma, though often depressed, grew stronger and the baby made gradual progress, so that arrangements were made for the christening.

My parents travelled from Hampshire, and Louise Victoria rose to the occasion by crying lustily throughout the service at the village church.

Even Greville, although not ashamed of his obvious disappointment that Emma had not borne him a son, became bewitched by his little daughter and appeared quite charming during my parents' stay of one week at Castle Grange.

When the subject of my departure was broached he smiled in a quizzical way at me and said: 'You are, I know, loath to leave us, Abbey. Emma, I'm sure would welcome your company through the winter, so why not stay on until the spring?'

'That's a lovely idea, Grev,' Emma agreed. 'Yes, Abbey, please do?'

My mother sighed disinterestedly.

'You may just as well, Abigail. You show no enthusiasm in the London scene, or indeed Society at all.

A great disappointment to your father, to be sure. Perhaps by the spring you'll have had enough of the country and will be pleased to let us find you a husband.'

'I prefer to find my own husband, Mother,' I pleaded, quietly.

'In this lonely part of the world—ugh!' my mother retorted.

Greville and Emma exchanged glances, and I wondered whether Greville didn't regret his suggestion now.

'There's no suitors in these parts,' he said. 'So if it's husband-seeking you're about, you'd best get back to Hampshire.'

'You should know me well enough now, Greville, to know that I have no such quests,' I began with tongue in cheek, knowing full well, that now my thoughts were constantly at Lyme Towers what other quest could I possibly have? It was true that I still loved the area as much as ever, but a fresh interest was incurred in Lyme Towers.

'I have no intention of husband-seeking now or ever,' I flung defiantly at Greville.

'Then stay if you will, Abbey.' His look dared me to accept, only serving to stir my contrariness.

'Thank you, then I shall be pleased to,' I said. 'At least for a few more weeks.'

Emma was genuinely delighted and my parents relieved, but Greville—he was, I felt certain, quite put about and had not been sincere in his invitation.

I went in the carriage as far as the Castle Inn to see my parents safely boarded on the coach, and bade them farewell as it rumbled off on its journey to Hampshire, a journey in which I was thankful not to be a participant.

I would not have readily admitted to anyone that my main interest was in Charles McClure, yet experienced a desolate feeling at the thought of returning to Hampshire with my parents without seeing Charles again, or indeed bidding goodbye to Hannah.

She had sent word to me after the ball that she hoped Emma and the baby were doing well, and that my absence had not caused too much distress, and she looked forward to seeing me again as soon as I was able to take an afternoon off.

So now, having had an early luncheon before my parents' departure, I set off light-heartedly through the village towards Lyme Towers.

There was a rawness in the early December day, but I felt no discomfort, only mounting excitement as the home of Charles McClure came into view.

I was apprehensive at passing through his grounds unaccompanied, but I knew of no other way to reach Hannah's cottage.

Would Charles be in the house, I wondered, working on the affairs of the estate with Edward Lacey? Might he be out riding and would accost me at any moment?—but I was disheartened, for I met no one.

Stealing a furtive glance towards the pillared balcony from across the lake, Lyme Towers was still magically attractive, even though there were no lights or gay music, as on the unforgettable night of the ball.

I could not be sure I was taking the right pathway, and there was no Humphrey to greet me this time, but as soon as the charming cottage came into view I knew I should receive a warm welcome.

Hannah must have seen me approaching, for the front door opened and she stood calmly with outstretched arms awaiting me.

'My dear Abbey. How delightful. Do come along in and warm yourself by the fire.'

I took off my bonnet and shawl as Hannah drew two armchairs nearer the fire. Why had I sensed a sadness before? I wondered, for now the cottage was cosy and inviting.

'Hannah, do please excuse my bad manners in not returning your dress long before this. Mrs. Thwaites has sponged and pressed it, I trust it is satifactory?'

'I had not even missed it, Abbey, but thank you all the same, and I am pleased that it gave you the excuse to call on me again.'

'There has been so much to do with Emma having the baby rather sooner than expected, and then my parents' arrival for the christening.'

'I trust your sister is well, Abbey, and the baby? A delight to you all, I'm sure.'

'Yes, she's sweet. Though Greville, of course, wanted a boy, and is somewhat disgruntled at the disappointment. Emma is about again, but suffering from a tiredness of the blood, so she has days of taking to her bed. Poor Emma, she does so long to resume social calls and parties. My parents are returning to Hampshire today, I have just seen them off on the midday coach.'

'And you have not gone with them?' Hannah seemed surprised.

'No, Greville asked me to stay on, though I fear he did not expect me to accept. My mother is still displeased with me, so I could think of no good reason to return home with them. I adore my little niece, so I mean to make the most of her and spoil her outrageously.'

'She is a lucky baby, and what are her names?'

'Louise Victoria.'

'How charming, a nice choice. So you are not yet tired of Devon, Abbey?'

'Indeed no. I am loath to leave at all, Hannah, now that I have made friends here.'

'It pleases me to hear you say that, my dear. You

quite obviously enjoyed the hunt ball. It was a grand affair, wasn't it? Mr. Charles knows how to entertain.'

'Lyme Towers is rather a grand place. Not as old as Castle Grange, I suspect?'

'Probably not, though little is known of the families and estates in these parts, owing to a fire at the agent's offices in Exeter over a century ago, destroying many of the important records, and local history. Poor Charles is having some difficulty in settling his affairs in order. It makes it a more arduous task too, on account of his not having lived here until recently, since he was a very young boy.'

Her cheeks had become quite pink at my instantaneous reaction when she dropped the 'Mr.' Charles for the first time.

What was there between them? Was she his mistress, or past lover? For a brief moment I felt uneasy, or might it not be jealousy?

The awkward silence was relieved by a sudden knocking on the window as Edward passed on his way to the back door.

'Hannah!' he cried, waving some papers. 'I've found it, dearest, this is great news. Charles is the . . . Oh, Miss Abigail, I do beg your pardon. I didn't realise Hannah had company.'

'I must apologise for being an uninvited guest,' I said hastily, wondering at the reason for his boyish fervour.

'Come now, Abbey. You *were* invited.' Hannah insisted. 'Edward, I was not expecting you. Will you join Abbey and me in a cup of tea?'

'Um, no. I've found some important documents, Hannah, and I am anxious to meet Charles at the very earliest moment.' He looked concerned now, and I suspected that he wished I was not present so that he could talk with his wife.

'I can come again, Hannah, if Edward . . . ?'

But Hannah silenced me with a wave of her hand.

'What time do you expect Charles back from Exeter, Edward?' she asked calmly.

'Not for another hour—I think I shall ride out to meet him, or perhaps wait at the inn.'

'You must be patient, dear. He will arrive in due course.'

'I can hardly contain myself, Hannah. Charles's journey to Exeter was quite unnecessary. My, there are still a great deal of papers to be consulted and sorted, and who knows what we may dig up before his father's estate is settled?' He tucked the papers away in an inside pocket of his long coat. 'I think I shall go as far as the inn, Hannah. I shall bring Charles back here with me—maybe a little celebration will be in order. Goodbye to you both.'

Hannah smiled as he left the cottage, and we heard him gallop away. She remained unmoved by his enthusiasm and presently prepared tea.

The minutes ticked by loudly on the handsome grandfather clock, each quarter-hour chiming, until not one hour but two had elapsed since Edward's departure.

Although I knew that Charles McClure's affairs were no business of mine, I was more than a little curious, and anxious to see him again, though by now darkness had enveloped the quiet countryside and Hannah had lit the lamp. I should have left while there was still daylight to see me back to Castle Grange, but something prevented me from leaving Hannah, and now I had left it too late. I should need someone to accompany me.

Another hour passed by, during which I helped Hannah with the tea things, after which she relaid the table for Edward.

At last the sound of a horse reached us, but there was no sign of Edward as Charles McClure entered the cottage, standing in the same spot as Edward had done, his face drawn.

At first he seemed unable to speak. Hannah stood up, her eyes meeting his, pleasure changing rapidly to concern.

'Hannah, my dear,' Charles said. 'I don't know how to tell you. Edward—there's been an accident. I'm sorry—Edward is dead.'

# Six

HANNAH'S GAZE did not leave Charles's face. A small muscle in one corner of her mouth twitched as she briefly wrung her hands together.

Then she moved silently to the table, picked up the china she had set and put it away on the oak dresser.

'He won't be needing tea then,' she muttered softly.

Unable to believe what I had heard or seen, I stood up and faced Charles.

'How awful!' I said. 'But how, Charles? What has happened?'

Charles had been watching Hannah. Now, as if noticing my presence for the first time, he took a stride towards me, placing both hands on my shoulders.

'Abbey, my dear Abbey. How glad I am that you're here.'

Hannah swung round, her voice breaking a little as she said: 'How did it happen, Charles?'

'Knocked down by a horse it seems. But, Hannah, what was Edward doing at the inn? He should have been working up at the house. I left him more than enough to keep him occupied for at least two days.'

'He was anxious to meet you,' Hannah said, her brow puckering a little as she sought to remember Edward's words. 'He found some documents of interest, and was quite excited by it, so he went down to the inn to await your arrival.'

Charles wiped his brow with his handkerchief and

paced up and down the small parlour, deep in thought.

'Documents—eh?' he muttered. 'So he heard a horseman approaching and presumed it was me. In the half-light I doubt if anyone saw who it was. I must return to the inn at once. Abbey—you will stay, please, because *I* am asking you?'

He clasped both my hands in his, and searched my eyes for agreement.

'Oh course, Charles. I shall not leave Hannah; but can word be sent to Emma?'

'Yes, my dear. Write a note to her to explain and I will get young Lucy's brother from the village to deliver it. Hannah, you know what to do? The coroner must be informed. Edward's body will be brought here.'

'I understand, Charles, and thank you,' Hannah said, handing me pen and paper.

'Edward has been a friend of long standing,' Charles said. 'You know I shall do all I can to help, but at this moment I must get back to retrieve the documents he had found, lest they fall into the wrong hands. Are you sure he had them with him and did not leave them here or at Lyme Towers?'

'Quite sure, Charles.' She gave a short laugh. 'But for Edward's boyish zest I might not have known he had found anything, but he just *had* to tell me.'

'Let us hope that drink did not loosen his tongue too much,' Charles said. 'Poor Edward, I am deeply grieved by this.'

He turned and left, bearing my brief note to Emma.

There was a painful silence as neither of us spoke or even looked at each other.

Then I went to Hannah.

'I'm so sorry, Hannah. What can I say?'

'Nothing, Abbey. We can alter nothing. To think

that Edward had travelled extensively with the military, only to be killed by a horse.'

'Surely the rider must have seen Edward? He would not be so foolish to walk in front of a horse?'

Hannah smiled wistfully.

'Who knows what happened? Edward was excited enough without the added drink which I'm sure he would have consumed while waiting for Charles. He may not have been capable of seeing how close the horseman was. But come, there are preparations to be made. A bed for you—are you sure you want to stay, Abbey? There's no real need.'

'Charles wanted me to, Hannah.'

'And you're fond of Charles, aren't you, Abbey?'

'That's of no matter at the present, Hannah,' I said, turning from her, hurt that she should choose that moment to comment upon my emotions.

We drew the curtains throughout the cottage, and after making room in the front parlour for the coffin to be rested, I helped Hannah spread the sheets on the big bed in the back bedroom for myself.

Then we sat down again by the fire to wait for the undertakers.

Hannah spoke little, and presently we heard the horse and cart coming through the lane. But Charles was back too and begged us to remain by the fire while he did all that was necessary.

'I could do with a drink, Hannah,' he said, after the men had left. 'Have you anything in the house?'

'Brandy?'

'Yes, that will do. Then I think we could all do with a cup of tea.'

Hannah's fingers trembled as she poured out the alcohol, then, as she gave it to Charles, she began to laugh.

'Edward said we'd have a celebration!' she screamed. 'He must have celebrated on his own.'

'Hannah! Control yourself. Abbey, perhaps you'd be good enough to make the tea.'

The kettle was already boiling on the hob on the fire. Charles drank his brandy in one gulp while Hannah's laughter became hysterical.

'Hannah!' Charles shouted. 'Hannah, please!' and he shook her fiercely.

She went quite limp in his grasp, then completely reverted to her normal self.

'Charles, forgive me—I'm sorry—I can't think what came over me,' she said quietly, and at once set the table for supper.

Charles stood near me as I filled the pot and whispered:

'It's the shock, I suppose.'

'Would you care for some bread and cheese, Charles?' Hannah asked.

'Yes, my dear. I would. I've had little to eat all day.'

Hannah and I remained by the fire drinking our cups of tea. We had no appetite for food, so Charles sat alone at the small round table to partake of the supper Hannah prepared for him.

When he had done with eating he poured himself another cup of tea and pulled his chair round facing the hearth.

'There were no documents on Edward's person,' he said, shortly.

Hannah looked from Charles to me.

'Abbey, Edward showed them to us, surely I was not mistaken?' she said.

'No,' I agreed. 'He had them in his hand and waved them in excitement.'

'There was nothing on him. No papers, no money. His pockets were empty.'

'Oh dear,' I said. 'I fear I should not have been here. I'm sure Edward would have consulted you on the matter in much more detail, Hannah. He would most likely have shown you the documents, but for my untimely call.'

'Abbey, now don't you get all of a state,' Charles said.

'Indeed no,' Hannah determined. 'It is most improbable that Edward would have allowed me to handle such important papers. I'm afraid, Abbey, he was not always as responsible as he might have been.'

'In this case, Hannah, Edward acted in good faith and I do assure you had but one glass of ale, so Matthew, the publican, assures me. Did he give you any hint of what the papers contained, Hannah?'

'None at all, excepting to say that your journey to Exeter was unnecessary after all.'

Charles sighed. 'This is indeed a bad business.'

'Was there no one at the inn to tell what happened?' Hannah asked.

'Only that he rushed out when he thought he heard me approaching. There's a strange silence about the place. A silence I don't care for.'

'Were there many people at the inn? It was still quite early.'

Charles didn't answer at first.

'I can't rightly say who was there. As I approached the inn I could see something in the ditch. I passed by and tethered Duke. As I said, I had had nothing to eat all day, so decided to take a meal at the inn. I glanced back wondering what it was in the ditch and realised it was a man's body.'

'So you found him—no one knew he was there?'

'Or didn't want to know, Hannah. The inn must have been all but empty when I entered, and Matthew—well, he seemed odd. I had to shout at him to get him to come, and help me carry Edward into the back room. When we discovered he was dead, Matthew sent his lad after the constable.'

'You think the horseman just rode off after knocking Edward down?' I ventured.

'That's how it looks, but it's my belief that he stopped and took all he wanted first. Most likely it was only the papers he really wanted, but he took the money to make it look like robbery.'

'A genuine hardened thief would have taken only his money,' Hannah said, 'the papers would have been insignificant to him.'

'But they were your documents, Charles,' I said. 'Why should anyone else want them, and how would they know that Edward had them?'

Charles sighed and glanced anxiously at Hannah.

'The whole business is very much involved, my dear Abbey, but I'll get to the bottom of it in the end. Now I must return to Lyme Towers. Hannah, have you somehing you can take to help you sleep?'

'I shall not need anything, but—I wonder, Charles—would you just take me in to see Edward before you go?'

'My dear, of course.'

Seeing that for the moment my presence was not required, I bade them both good night and went upstairs, assuring Hannah that she had only to call if she could not sleep, or needed me for anything.

It was strange in the small cottage to be able to hear their movements and low hum of their voices, unlike the large rooms in the houses to which I was accustomed.

I lay listening, and wondering. Surely, after her laughter Hannah *must* shed tears.

But she was a strong-minded woman, and I suspected refused to allow her emotions to engulf her.

Unless—unless she preferred to show her emotions to the man of whom, I was confident, she was a little more than fond.

What was I thinking of? Here, under the same roof as Hannah and her dead husband, and already my thoughts were exploring the future!

But I could not sleep for the torturing nightmares. What were the feelings of Charles? Was his charm bestowed upon every woman who perchanced his way?

Did Edward's death provide a happy solution for his and Hannah's hidden feelings?

For the first time in my life I believed myself to be in love. Although as yet I knew little enough of Charles McClure, my pulse quickened at the sound of his name; his presence caused a great upsurge of emotion within me such as I had never hitherto experienced.

And now—with one blow—my desires had to be suppressed.

After Charles had left I watched for the quivering reflection of candlelight which would bring Hannah to her room. But it did not come, and the cottage became enveloped in silent mourning.

Weariness must have given way to sleep, for the next thing I knew was Hannah standing by my bed with a tray in her hand.

It took a moment to recall the events which had led to my being in Hannah's home. She was dressed now in a dark grey dress with black lace, and a black silk shawl.

'Hannah!' I exclaimed, still heavy with sleep. 'You should have called me earlier. Did you manage to have a little sleep?'

'A little, Abbey. There was nothing to call you for,

my dear. Charles's concern was quite without foundation.'

'But it is I who should have brought you a breakfast tray,' I said, helplessly.

'I'm quite used to being alone, Abbey. Edward's military service took him away a great deal. Please, have your breakfast at leisure before dressing.'

But as I hastily set aside the tray and dressed I felt sure that Hannah had not even been to bed.

I ate and drank in between dressing and brushing my hair, feeling guilty at having slept so soundly for the latter half of the night. Above all, should Charles decide to pay an early call, I did not wish him to think me selfish in sleeping on.

We had cleared the breakfast things when the parson arrived, and while he and Hannah went into the front parlour, I went outside to draw water from the pump.

When I returned to the back door Charles arrived with Humphrey at his heels.

'Good morning, Abbey. How is Hannah this morning?'

'The parson is here,' I told him in a low voice, as he followed me into the cottage. 'Hannah seems so—so . . .'

'Calm— independent?' he suggested.

'Yes—if only she would let herself go, Charles.'

'But that wouldn't be Hannah. She is a woman apart,' he said, a tone of admiration creeping in. 'Her undignified laughter is probably the only show of emotion you will see, my dear.'

'I am here,' I said with a shrug, 'but she doesn't need me. In fact, I fancy she might prefer to be alone.' I looked away from his haunting dark eyes, ashamed at my discernment.

He lifted my chin gently.

'*I* asked you to stay. You did it for me, Abbey. Thank you. Hannah has no relatives, neither had Edward in this locality. So, I am going to ask you another favour. As Hannah's friend—as *my* friend—would you be gracious enough to attend Edward's funeral? There will only be the three of us.'

'Well, I hardly knew Edward, but if Hannah wants . . .'

'*I* want,' he interrupted. 'It would hardly be ethical for Hannah's only other chief mourner to be me alone.'

His implication needed no further explanation. My eyes flashed angrily towards him as I tossed my head in defiance. He was using me to prevent gossip! Why hadn't I seen through his little game before?

But I had no chance to tell him what I thought, for Hannah emerged with the parson.

'Ah, Miss Rothesay, Mr. McClure.' The parson was a thin, spiky-looking man with a very flushed face and beady eyes. 'I'm so pleased that Mrs. Lacey has a few friends to rally round at a time like this. Such a tragedy.'

He shook hands with each of us in turn, then Hannah took him to the front door.

'There are a few details to attend to, Hannah, my dear,' Charles said, after he had left. 'No doubt a few local people will wish to pay their respects, so as Abbey is anxious to return to Castle Grange I shall send the carriage for her.'

'I'm quite capable of walking,' I said, unable to hide the edge to my voice.

He looked down at me, a merry twinkle shining momentarily from his eyes.

'I said, I'll send the carriage. What would your sister think of me if I allowed you to trudge back through the village, after your kindness in staying to accompany Hannah?'

'Yes, Abbey, I am most grateful,' Hannah intervened. 'But now that the first shock of Edward's death has passed, I must get used to being independent.'

'If you're sure,' I said softly.

'Abbey is coming to the funeral, Hannah,' Charles told her. 'It will be the day after tomorrow. I shall, of course, send my carriage for you, Abbey.'

Hannah's eyes seemed to open wider, but she quickly recovered, saying: 'Oh—oh, yes, thank you, Charles,' before I could speak, but I perceived that the arrangement had been made without her knowledge.

'I'll go tidy my room then, if there's nothing more I can do for you,' I said.

Suddenly I wanted to go home to my sister. I didn't understand the situation in which I found myself. It was as if I wanted to cry for Edward if no one else would.

How stupidly vulnerable I'd been, and I thought I was shrewd enough to see through people like Charles and Hannah.

Arriving back at Castle Grange, I met only Mrs. Thwaites and told her I should go to my room to change for luncheon.

But once alone I gave way to a deluge of tears, and hated myself for doing so.

I had been foolishly feminine enough to fall in love, so now I had to behave just as Emma would have done. Oh, how I hated men! I beat my fists on the chair and cried in utter despair.

But it was not my nature to behave thus, and I soon dried my eyes, and washed and changed.

It refreshed me to see and nurse Louise Victoria before luncheon was ready, and while I sat with her a firm hand was placed upon my shoulder.

'Abbey, I understand there's been some trouble on the McClure estate?'

I turned in surprise at the recognition of Greville's voice.

'Well, not really trouble on the estate,' I said. 'Hannah's husband, Edward, was knocked down and killed outside the Castle Inn.'

'How very distressing. Did no one see what occurred?'

'No—he was waiting at the inn for Mr. McClure, and, thinking the horseman was he, Edward ran out, I believe.'

'I am shocked, Abbey, and would be grateful if you would pass on my sincere condolences to Mrs. Lacey. I expect you'll be attending the funeral?'

'Yes. I have been asked to, as Hannah has no relatives.'

'When is it to be?'

'The day after tomorrow.'

'And do you require a new dress or shawl?'

I could hardly believe this new attitude from my brother-in-law.

'Thank you, Greville, but I have a suitable black dress and shawl,' I assured him.

During luncheon Greville talked quite amicably of the affair, and showed a genuine concern for Hannah.

Afterwards he came to the drawing room with several lengths of material hanging over his arm. To my astonishment I saw that they were not black silk as I expected, but gay patterns.

'Come, my dear, and you, Abbey, choose a bright new dress to cheer yourselves up for Christmas.'

'Greville!' Emma cried delightedly, and each length was held up against her to see which suited her best, and it was Emma who picked a suitable one for me.

Now that I was back at Castle Grange I began to see things differently, and felt I had been hasty in my judgement of Charles and Hannah.

I was pleased to be considered one of Hannah's friends and could see the awkward position she was in with no family of her own.

The morning of the funeral was dry but cold, and Hannah looked pale as heavily veiled she followed the bearers, after the short service in the parish church, to the open grave.

The parson's intonations were barely audible in the bleak graveyard, and Charles too looked drawn.

Later, as I travelled back to Castle Grange, alone in the McClure carriage, I felt extremely sad, but also mystified at the lack of emotion from Hannah. She had not wept at all, and during the refreshments back at the cottage she seemed almost gay.

# Seven

THE COURSE OF EVENTS caused me to feel depressed, and I spent the remainder of the day quietly and alone until Emma insisted that I should sit with her in the evening.

'A funeral is always dampening to one's spirits, Abbey,' she said, 'even if you hardly knew the person. How did Hannah take it?'

'Exceedingly well, Emma, I cannot understand it. She has not shed a tear for her own husband. It is one thing not to give way to needless weeping, but to be so strong-minded at such a time as this seems quite heartless to me.'

'But it was all so sudden, Abbey. I doubt that the poor woman realises yet that her husband is gone. Hannah strikes me as being a cold woman. Oh, gentle and well bred, I am sure, but she has an austere manner.'

'I must visit her often during the coming days,' I mused, 'in case she feels she needs someone to talk with.'

'I imagine Charles McClure will be a frequent visitor,' Emma said, glancing across at me. 'There has already been gossip concerning them, Abbey, and they only took up residence on the estate a few months ago.'

'Charles and Edward were old friends, so I understand,' I said, hastily trying to excuse any undue interest in Charles.

I almost wished now that I had returned to Hampshire with my parents, yet I knew that however much I had to suffer because of Charles and Hannah's relationship, I should be compelled to visit Hannah often in the hope of a chance meeting with Charles.

A few mornings later, after the baby had been attended to, and could safely be left in Lucy's care, I went with Emma to the village in the carriage, the reason being an assignation with the proprietors of the drapery store.

The Misses Bell were awaiting our arrival with eagerness.

'Good morning, Mrs. Bond. A nice morning, although rather colder, and how is your little one?' the slightly taller of the two sisters enquired. I could never remember which of them was which, so was grateful that Miss Bell sufficed for either.

'Good day to you both,' Emma replied. 'Louise is adorable, of course, and doing very nicely now.'

I had nodded my greeting and noticed that the two sisters were inquisitively eyeing the parcel I was carrying.

The smaller of the two Miss Bells, and the younger, I fancied, hovered nervously from one side of her sister to the other, so Emma wasted no time in stating the reason for our appointment.

'My husband has purchased lengths of material for my sister and myself, and wishes us to have them made up in time for Christmas. Do you think you can manage that, Miss Bell?'

'Why yes, Mrs. Bond, of course we shall be happy to oblige,' the taller Miss Bell assured Emma.

'Delighted, I'm sure,' the other echoed, as her sister almost pushed her aside to open a glass-panelled door at the rear of the shop, across which was painted: 'WORKSHOP'.

Emma followed Miss Fanny Bell, and behind me pranced the shorter sister.

At their request we removed our shawls and the efficient Miss Fanny measured each of us in turn. We selected our styles and then Emma opened the parcel. The two little women gasped at the beauty of the fabric.

The smaller sister, Miss Hetty, fingered each piece and kept glancing up at her sister with a little 'Oh—oh!'

'Beautiful,' agreed Miss Fanny, 'and you didn't buy this hereabouts, I'll be bound?'

Emma's smile was, I thought, a trifle forced as she said, non-committally:

'I told you, it's a present from my husband.'

'Fine *French* taffeta, which cost a pretty penny or my name's not Fanny Bell!'

'Oh—oh!' muttered Miss Hetty again, and Emma hastened to explain her exact requirements.

The doorbell clanged an interruption and as Miss Hetty gathered up her skirt and hurried back to the shop, I was alarmed at the way her sister pushed the lengths of taffeta back into the parcel and out of sight.

It wasn't until we were in the carriage again that the truth dawned on me. *French* taffeta, Miss Fanny had suggested. Where would Greville obtain such luxuries but from the source Mrs. Thwaites had spoken of?

'I think I shall call on Hannah!' I told Emma, acting upon a sudden, more wholesome impulse.

'Yes, all right, Abbey, she'll be pleased to see you. We'll drive round to her cottage and I'll tell Sam to wait a while to make sure your visit is convenient.'

But to my dismay the cottage seemed deserted.

There was no sign of Hannah, or Humphrey, but just as I stepped back into the carriage a young fair-haired youth rode up to us. He raised his cap politely.

'Mrs. Lacey is up at the big house, miss,' he said. 'She saw the carriage pass the lake, and would have you join her at Lyme Towers, where you will be welcome to stay to luncheon.'

I felt my body retract as if I was hiding from reality. What was Hannah doing at Lyme Towers, and why should she be anxious for me to join her when she could have Charles all to herself?

Or was I being used again?

Emma looked at me curiously as I hesitated. Could she read my thoughts?

'We can drop you off, Abbey,' she said. 'You can't refuse an invitation like that.'

'No—no.' I turned to the young man. 'Tell Mrs. Lacey I shall be pleased to join her.'

The youth rode off, and I sat pensively as Sam turned the carriage on the green before setting off towards the majestic Lyme Towers, which quickly became visible as we drove round the lake.

'Abbey—dear,' Emma whispered gently, 'do be careful. I fear you are going to be terribly hurt.'

'Hurt?'

Emma smiled. 'It's not my affair, but I can see that you have become very fond of Charles McClure. It's a great pity that he holds Hannah Lacey in such high esteem. Who can say if such a man is capable of really loving any woman.'

'I am calling on Hannah,' I replied pertly. 'I doubt that I shall even see Charles.'

Emma patted my hand in a motherly fashion.

'Enjoy your day, dear, but if you walk home, please set off well before dark.'

As the carriage pulled up, Hannah was standing at the door waiting. She waved to Emma as I mounted the steps, and the carriage went on its way.

'Abbey, this is a delightful surprise. I'm so sorry I wasn't at the cottage.'

'How are you, Hannah?' I expected to see some sign of strain, but she looked as composed as ever. 'I wondered if you might be feeling lonely, and in need of company.'

'You are *so* thoughtful, Abbey. I am well enough, and with little time for feeling lonely as I have agreed to continue with some of the work Edward had undertaken for Charles.'

'Oh, Hannah!' I exclaimed, quite taken aback. 'Are things so bad that you must work?'

I had removed my bonnet and shawl, and now followed Hannah into a room off the hall.

A huge table was scattered with books and papers, but Hannah directed me to an armchair near the log fire.

'Come sit down, luncheon will be served to us here, on a small table where we can be more comfortable.'

Hannah was dressed again in the plain grey dress. Her hair neat as always, and her cheeks waxlike, but still the dove-grey eyes showed no sign of emotion.

She must have sensed my feelings as I stared at her.

'I'm glad to have something to do, Abbey,' she explained. 'And even more glad to be of some assistance to Charles. I am not working in the sense of a servant, but rather as a friend helping a friend.'

'Oh, I see. You're right, of course, Hannah. It is better to keep occupied,' I agreed.

'With Edward in the Army and frequently away from home it is not a new experience for me to be alone.'

'But you always had Edward's home-coming to look forward to before,' I said, trying to convey some sympathy.

Hannah smiled, and refrained from answering until

the maid had left the room after placing a tray on the small table between us.

'I expect, Abbey, you must think me quite heartless. I do not show my emotions easily; indeed, over the years I have had to learn to hide my deepest feelings.'

'But surely, Hannah, that is not good?' I protested.

Hannah smiled. 'You are young, Abbey, and I hope will never have to endure the unhappiness I've had to live with."

'Unhappiness?' I echoed. 'Were you not happy with Edward?'

Hannah slowly removed the lid from a large brown stewpot and served some delicious rabbit stew to me.

'In all marriages there are happy and unhappy times, my dear. You see, Abbey, our marriage was an arranged one between families. We had to learn to love each other just a little to make life tolerable, even though our real desires lay elsewhere.

'I didn't know,' I gasped. 'I'm sorry, Hannah.'

'That's all right, Abbey. It was all some twelve years ago, and I was betrothed to Edward on my eighteenth birthday. Edward had some endearing ways, and we made the best of an impossible situation.'

'Did Edward really love someone else then?' I asked.

'Edward loved all beautiful creatures, but more than women, he loved money. But for Charles's constant help I'm afraid Edward's gambling debts would have put him in gaol many times.'

'How distressing for you, Hannah!'

'Distressing, yes,' she sighed. 'But frustrating for Edward too, I fear. I was never able to bear him the son he longed for, which perhaps helped to drive him to drink and gambling. Being abroad a great deal made him an easy victim for confidence tricksters. Charles paid many a debt on Edward's behalf and saved him perhaps from worse pastimes—who can say? When Charles inherited Lyme Towers at first he thought he would sell up because he was devoted to serving his country, and I fancy felt some alliance to Edward for my sake. But he brought us here to see the estate, and it became obvious that it revived old and happy childhood memories, so I persuaded him to take up his rightful place as heir.'

'And you came too?'

'It was Charles's idea after he had been here only a short while. I didn't try to persuade Edward one way or the other, and I must admit it came as a surprise when he accepted the offer. But Edward had depended upon Charles too long, so, there was no one here really suitable to act as agent, and the estate had been somewhat neglected, Charles decided Edward was the right person to help him manage it. We were delighted with the way he had prepared the cottage for us and for the first time in our marriage Edward really seemed to enjoy his work. Like Charles, he regarded it as a challenge.'

I didn't answer at first. There was so much I wanted to know about the McClure family and Charles, but didn't want my curiosity to seem impertinent.

'It would seem a great shame to give up a worthwhile military career if he was really dedicated,' I said, 'but if he is the only son, I suppose he had little choice?'

'Charles is the only child, as indeed his father was before him. He too was a military man in his younger days. For several years now the estate has been allowed to drift along without proper management and Charles is anxious to make it a going concern once he can get things straightened out. As you can see, we are going back over the records in detail.'

Again I fell silent, following Hannah's gaze to the

volume of paper work covering the table, wondering to what purpose it was necessary to delve back into the past, when it would seem working to make the estate profitable was of more importance.

A sniffing and pawing at the door preceded the arrival of the maid bringing another plate and extra cutlery. Charles entered close behind, at his heel the faithful Humphrey.

'Abbey, this is an unexpected pleasure,' he said, clasping my hand in a firm, warm handshake.

'I must apologise if I am hindering the work here,' I told him. 'I called at the cottage thinking Hannah might be lonely.'

'There is nothing so important here that Hannah cannot entertain her friends. We are both delighted to welcome you at Lyme Towers.'

Inwardly I flinched at the 'we are both', and sadly wondered how long would elapse before Hannah would take her place as the lady of Lyme Towers. No one could be more suitable, of course, for such a distinguished position and Charles would be anxious to make up to Hannah for Edward's past misdemeanors.

'I hope the stew is to your liking, Abbey,' Charles was saying. 'I like fresh country food, such a contrast to Army meals. This young rabbit was caught soon after dawn this morning.'

'It is quite delicious,' I agreed.

'Partly due to Charles's competent cook,' Hannah explained.

'Yes, you must come and meet Oliver some time, Abbey. A frightening fellow to look at—big and very black, every inch a Negro, but at heart as docile as a lamb.'

'Where on earth did you find such a fellow?' I asked.

'Oh, on my travels abroad. He'd had a lean time of it, and because I befriended him he clung to me as my slave, so I had to find him some really useful work to do, and have endeavoured to teach him some self-respect.'

'Charles is a veritable Good Samaritan,' Hannah said, with a smile.

'Not really,' Charles said, his tanned cheeks crinkling with laughter lines. 'But I do believe in loyalty among friends.'

I sensed that Hannah stiffened at his words, but I paid no heed at the time as she asked:

'And how is that niece of yours, Abbey?'

I smiled readily.

'A little darling, and getting quite sturdy now. She will take after her mother in looks, I think, already her fine hair has a golden sheen to it.'

'I can see she will be thoroughly indulged by her young aunt,' Charles said.

'And why not? That's what I came here for.'

'That's not what you told me when we first met, Abbey,' Hannah said, a twinkle in her eyes. 'I believe it was an Earl you were running away from?'

'Yes,' I laughed. 'I'd quite forgotten him, though my parents haven't, I fear.'

'And what type of man shall you marry, Abbey?' Charles asked.

My cheeks turned very pink even though I knew Charles was only teasing, but before I could reply the sound of raised voices reached us from the hall, saving me any further embarrassment.

The door burst open and the young maid curtsied to Charles in a flustered fashion.

'Mr. McClure, sir, 'tis big Matt Yates from the inn. Wants to see you, he does, sir.'

An enormous man barged awkwardly into the room, giving the maid a not-too-gentle push.

Charles rose to his feet instantly, almost sending the plates and stewpot to the floor.

' 'Tis no good, Mr. McClure, I can't bide and hold me tongue no longer. 'Tis no good Mr. Bond trying to bribe me neither.'

'Matthew, come outside, please—the ladies . . .'

Charles caught at the innkeeper's arm, but the big, burly man, red-faced and puffing, refused to be silenced.

'I must say what I come to say, sir, and it concerns Mrs. Lacey there. Begging your pardon, ma'am. 'Twere a terrible thing what happened to your good man—an' I must tell the truth, even though Mr. Bond wanted to pay me to say that he wasn't in the inn that night.'

'Matthew,' Charles interjected in a loud voice, 'this is Miss Rothesay—Mr. Bond's sister-in-law.'

The blustering Matthew stopped and gulped, looking at me as if he saw me for the first time. I nodded toward him, though by now I felt convinced that it would have been better for everyone if I had not been at Lyme Towers.

An awkward silence ensued, then Matthew Yates pulled himelf up, attempting to shrink his enormous stomach as if it would add to his already ample inches.

'I'm sorry, sir—miss—but I *must* speak. Mr. Lacey came to the inn that night for a glass of ale, and said as how he were waiting for Mr. McClure to return from Exeter. Good news, he had, he said, concerning the estate and land hereabouts. There was only one or two other men at the inn, and one of them was Mr. Bond, who seemed bothered by Mr. Lacey's excitement, and so he soon left. About half an hour later we heard a horse approaching fast. 'Twere getting dark and Mr. Lacey ran outside to stop you, sir, passing by. We heard him shout, and the horseman stopped, but then a few minutes later rode off again.

When Mr. Lacey didn't come back into the inn we thought as how he'd gone home, though 'tweren't like him to leave his ale unsupped. Then, of course, you knows what happened, sir, 'cos you found the poor man.'

Charles ran his fingers through his hair.

'Thank you, Matt,' he said quietly. 'I already had my suspicions.'

'I've said me piece, now I'll have done, and get back to the inn and get on with my work. You do whatever you think best, Mr. McClure, sir, for 'tis my belief it weren't no accident. A bit of smuggling's one thing, but this was murder!'

'But we have no evidence, Matt, and never will have, unless those papers come to light. If only Edward had left them here.'

Charles ushered the innkeeper out. By this time I was sitting uncomfortably on the edge of the chair. What did all this mean? I looked questioningly at Hannah, but she sat motionless, her slender hands clasped in her lap.

Charles returned and closed the door firmly.

'I'm sorry about that, Abbey. It would have been better if Matthew had chosen a more convenient time.'

I stood up and faced Charles.

'When I wasn't here, you mean, because he has implicated that Greville is responsible for Edward's death. I am deeply shocked, Charles, but do not understand why.'

Charles beat one fist into the other palm, and paced the room.

'Abbey,' he said, slowly, 'we are doing our best to recover what rightfully belongs to the Lyme Towers estate—namely, the ruins and land of the old monastery which your brother-in-law claims belongs to Castle Grange and which he uses for smuggling.'

'But what has that to do with Edward's death?' I asked.

'You were at Hannah's cottage when Edward called in saying he had found some documents. I believe they were very important, probably throwing some light on the inheritance of the monastery grounds.'

'But Greville wouldn't have known that,' I said.

'Matthew said that Edward was excited. Greville Bond would have been a worried man at that moment.'

'But he wouldn't kill a man for such a reason.'

Charles looked at me with troubled eyes.

'Not deliberately, Abbey—I hope, but he meant to see those documents before I did.'

'You think he took everything—from poor Edward's body?' I exclaimed.

'Who else? No one but your brother-in-law and myself would be interested.'

'And what would he want to do with them?'

'Possibly destroy them, unfortunately, which means I may never be able to settle this dispute—unless, he has them and anything else he may have taken from Edward at Castle Grange.' He paused, and looked at Hannah. 'And you, Abbey . . . ?'

'No, Charles, no!' Hannah cried 'Leave Abbey out of this.'

'She is already involved, I fear,' Charles said. 'But you are right, my dear, the idea is preposterous.'

'It certainly is,' I snapped, guilt coupled with shame causing me to lose control. 'I cannot remain here and listen to such accusations against my sister's husband when you have no proof. I'll trouble you for my bonnet and shawl, Hannah!'

# *Eight*

THE KEEN NORTH-EASTERLY WIND stung my burning cheeks as I hurried from Lyme Towers, and still ringing in my ears echoed Hannah and Charles's pleading to stay and talk.

But loyalty, I told myself, must be to Emma. Even though I disliked her husband I couldn't bring myself to believe he was capable of such a foul deed.

And yet just what had I thought on the night of the ball, when I had returned to Castle Grange? Emma's shriek had soon set my imagination to work. Just how ruthless could Greville Bond be?

Back at Castle Grange I tried to appear as if nothing had happened, which wasn't too difficult, as the long walk had relieved some of the tension.

'I didn't expect you back yet, Abbey,' Emma said with surprise.

'Hannah was busy,' I replied, indifferently.

'Doing what?'

'Oh, helping to sort out papers and old records, or something of the kind. She's continuing the work Edward was doing.'

'Working?'

'That was my reaction too, but she assures me she is only helping Charles. He has been more than a friend to her and Edward, so this is her way of repaying him.'

Emma sighed. 'Perhaps it is as well she has something to do. Life must seem without a purpose for her with no husband or family.'

'She is used to being alone, as Edward was away from home frequently, being in the Army,' I explained.

I took my bonnet and shawl to my room, and joined Emma later for tea, after which we spent an enjoyable hour with Louise Victoria.

But after she had been put to bed I had time to think again and found myself skeptical of Greville's every movement.

Supposing he had taken the documents? Had Charles really expected me to ask him for them, or search the house? The idea certainly was preposterous, and yet I found my shrewd eyes glancing at any likely papers left lying around.

I remembered Greville's concern at Edward's death. His attitude had become kind and he had been quite charming to me. Was it self-satisfaction at having found and destroyed some evidence that might have been to the benefit of Charles McClure?

Since generously giving us the material for our new gowns, though, he had very much reverted to his usual sullen self, hardly sparing so much as a look at his daughter, and little more for his wife; indeed we saw him only at meal-times.

As soon as I was able, after supper without causing undue attention, I sought refuge in my room.

It was not often I sat in the big comfy rocker, but tonight with a cold wind whistling round the turrets and tall chimneys I pulled it closer to the fire, extinguishing the candles and enjoying the solitude of the firelight.

Yet there was no enjoyment in it, nor in my own company, for I was miserable as I reflected over the day's events, wishing that I had gone home to Hampshire sooner. At least I would have gone still cherishing the friendship of Hannah and Charles—now, everything was spoilt.

I had been rude enough to leave Lyme Towers haughtily—I could never be invited back.

The evening turned into night as I rocked gently to and fro, watching the diminishing firelight flicker and dwindle till only an occasional reflection danced upon the ceiling.

The wind howled and died, and suddenly I heard a voice calling me.

'Abbey—Abbey—come quickly.'

I jumped up and ran to the window in response to the voice I was certain was Charles's, but his name faded on my lips as I realised it couldn't be. He wouldn't know which room I occupied, let alone the absurdity of his coming to Castle Grange at this late hour.

Wearily I turned away from the window, believing I had been dreaming, when the voice came again much clearer now.

'Abbey, Abbey—to the beach.'

I couldn't bear the agony of it. The voice had the gentle tone I so admired in Charles, and yet I knew it wasn't him.

I opened the window and peered out into the darkness. It was frosty and crisp with a bright moon.

'Abbey, Abbey.' There it was again.

'Who is it?' I called. 'Who's there?'

Then with a gasp I drew back as the monk appeared, suspended, it seemed, at the cliff edge just as I had seen him the very first time.

He had one finger to his lips, then he beckoned me.

'Come, Abbey. Follow me.'

Without a moment's hesitation I put on my warmest boots, shawl and over that a large thick cloak which had an atached hood.

Stealthily I crept out on to the landing—the house was sleeping and no candles or lamps were lit, but through the high windows the moon's reflections were sufficient for me to see. In any case I had been sitting so long with only the firelight that my eyes were accustomed to the semi-darkness.

But reaching the huge front door I stopped, knowing that I couldn't reach to draw back the enormous bolt that secured it.

The kitchen—yes, that would be the easiest way out. I opened a door leading from the hall and went down a flight of twisted stairs. There was no landing window here to reflect any light, but I knew this way, having visited Maud frequently when going on my long walks.

In the kitchen only an eery bluish light shone from the upper part of the high windows, showing the outline of the black-leaded stoves and huge ranges, but I managed to work my way round the wooden tables standing in the centre of the stone floor to the door, and to my surprise found it unlocked. Obviously the servants had a use for an unlocked door at night too!

Reaching the side of the house at the top of the stone steps I paused as the biting wind took my breath away.

Only when I had turned the corner and saw the glistening frost on the lawns did I wonder what madness had possessed me.

But there at the end of the terrace where the pathway led to the lane leading to the shingle beach was my friend the monk.

Friend? Surely he could mean me no harm with a voice so soft and gentle, reminding me of the man I loved?

I hurried along the terrace, hoping my crunching footsteps would not be heard, anxious to reach him, to talk to him, to find out whether he was merely a figment of my imagination or a real human being.

But always the shrouded figure remained ahead of me, close enough for me to feel his presence and yet far enough that I could not touch him.

With the sound of the heavy waves breaking over the large shingle I soon reached the end of the lane and turned on to the beach.

Meeting the wind again, I was forced to partially cover my face with my hood and walk as close to the undercliff as possible to gain some shelter from the bracken.

Every few yards I would look up, convinced that I should find myself alone, but the figure of the robed monk remained just ahead of me.

My feet became heavy, and walking slower as I battled against the elements, hobbling over the large pebbles.

'Who are you?' I called, trying once more to make contact. 'Where are we going?'

There was a pause. I stopped walking and for a split second it seemed that the man stood close to me.

'Don't be afraid, Abbey. You are safe with me. Come!'

'But why?' I insisted. 'It's the middle of the night, and it's freezing. What do you want with me?'

I put my hand out as if to grasp his clothes in the hope of restraining him, but there was nothing there; yet the same soft voice whispered on the wind:

'Just follow me, Abbey—Abbey. Something you must see for yourself.'

Irritated, but still determined to follow, I gathered my cloak more tightly round me and began walking again, noticing that the apparition was once more silhouetted against the moonlight.

It seemed as if I walked for hours, surely we should soon be at the monastery ruins. Was that our destination? Was that this monk's retreat?

I was anxious to visit the old monastery but had not anticipated doing so in the dead of night.

We must be near now, for frequently there were large boulders on the shingle beach, and glancing out to sea I observed that the coast became rugged as the beach narrowed. Ahead of me the cliff above jutted out against the skyline, a formation of rock descending to the beach moulding a natural doorway.

Suddenly I felt an arresting clutch at my arm.

'Listen, Abbey!'

Sheltering near the bushes, I tilted back my hood so that I could hear more distinctly the rough sea, and the thunderous rattle of pebbles as the water receded, and as the noise faded I heard the unmistakable crunch, crunch of footsteps on the shingle behind me, somewhere in the distance.

Someone else was taking a moonlight walk along the beach!

Another high wave broke on the shore, preventing me from concentrating on the approaching pursuer, but I felt myself being guided into the bushes.

'Hide, Abbey—quickly,' came the ghostlike voice, and as I stealthily concealed myself among the undergrowth I heard another strange sound—the splash, splash of oars hitting the water.

Curiosity urged me to turn back and peer seawards, but as I hesitated the grip tightened on my arm and I was gently persuaded to follow a pathway through the dense bushes of the undercliff, upwards and away from the beach. But only for a short distance.

'Wait here, you cannot be seen. Watch now, Abbey.'

My invisible protector had conducted me to an excellent vantage point about a third of the way up the cliff path. Sheltered from the wind, hidden from view and with the comforting thought that I was not entirely alone, I tossed the hood from my head and kept vigil.

With each lull of the breaking waves I could hear the crunch of footsteps getting closer, and as I watched towards the horizon I could just make out the profile of a large vessel anchored in the bay. Scanning the water nearer the beach, I could also see a small boat struggling against the wind and waves towards the shore.

It was making but little progress and I feared it would be dashed against the rocks as it wove its treacherous course.

The footsteps were closer now, yet it seemed an age before the low murmur of voices preceded the appearance of two figures just below me.

The cursory shouting of the men in the rowing boat reached me clearly as they fought their way to the water's edge, and as the two men crossed the beach to meet it, one of them turned and scrutinised the cliff.

I held my breath as I recognised Greville, my brother-in-law, but once more felt the reassuring hand upon my shoulder.

'Queer feel about the place tonight, Sam,' Greville said. 'As if someone's getting too curious.'

'Ah—'tis only that there ghost, sir. Won't have no peace in these parts till he's been laid,' the coach man declared.

'Hold your tongue, man,' Greville snapped, and looked about him anxiously. 'You and your silly superstitions, ghost indeed! Get there and help 'em to heave to. The sea's mighty angry tonight.'

Sam did as he was told and while Greville watched superciliously the boat was pulled inland.

Barrels and crates were unloaded and counted, then

each man paid in coins by my brother-in-law, before he handed round a flask, presumably of brandy.

I noticed a small dwarf-like man creeping round the bow of the rowing boat, but Greville's quick cunning spotted him too, just as he hid something under his coat.

'Scoundrel!' Greville roared, as with a savage blow he sent the man backwards into the icy water. 'Don't I pay you enough as it is—and little do I get in return, not even honesty?'

He waded in after the spluttering victim and hoisted him up by his coat collar. Sam emptied the man's pockets.

'Only two small bottles, sir,' he ventured.

'Only?' Greville shouted. 'And why should he have more than the rest—or have you all got something hidden away?'

All the men shifted about uneasily except Sam who stood fearlessly before Greville.

'No, sir. We all get paid enough, but poor 'ole Job, sir, his mother, and missus, and three of the kids are all took bad with the fever. We agreed he could have it—it might do 'um some good.'

'You all agreed, did you?' he sneered. 'Well, next time—ask! *I'll* decide what goes to the sick—if anything.'

He towered over the shivering little man, Job, as he struggled to his feet.

Greville handed him one of the bottles, and put the other in his own pocket.

'I'm not a bad man, Job. You should have told me about your family. There was no need for you to have turned out tonight.'

'But . . . but . . . I need the money, Mr. Bond, sir.'

'Then get on with the work—all of you,' Greville

shouted, and immediately barrels were hoisted up on shoulders and crates tugged across the stones as they started to come in my direction.

The hand had gone from my shoulder. I was alone, and surely must be discovered!

Panic seized me. Why were they coming this way? Why had the ghost left me here?

Frantically I pulled the hood up over my head, and wrapping my cloak tightly round me gathered up my skirts and turned to run.

The pathway showed up clearly in the frosty moonlight and I was soon weaving my way in and out among the bushes gaining the summit easily.

But reaching the headland I saw that the path divided off, one way leading on to the cliff edge, the other away under the cliff to the left.

I recognised the broken wall where the storm had driven me back from the cliff edge and shortly afterwards I had met Charles McClure, but I had no time for reflections, the men below were already climbing the path behind me. Should I follow the narrow track under the cliff and hope that it would lead me back to Castle Grange, or should I go back across the open headland?

I decided to take the route with which I was already vaguely familiar, but found difficulty in finding enough footholds to clamber over the broken wall.

But it was easier than I had expected when the soothing voice whispered in my ear:

'This way, Abbey—just relax and you will be safe, safe . . .' and as the voice died away on the wind it was as if I was being carried along, across the meadows with amazing speed until the turrets of Castle Grange loomed closer as I drew nearer home.

The night was cold and still again. Where had the men gone, for there were no voices to be heard now?

I crept into the silent house, up to my room and swiftly snuggled down in the feather bed, unable to believe the adventurous escapade was real. Yet the scene I had witnessed was too vivid to be anything but real.

My brother-in-law was a bullying task-master, a scheming smuggler who gained wealth from other people's misfortunes.

What was the ghost trying to convey to me?

That Greville Bond was capable of murder to perpetrate his own ends? And I had defended him—but only for Emma's sake.

How much of Greville's activities did Charles know? I wondered.

My thoughts became melancholy as I realised that however much I loved Charles the situation was quite impossible so long as the two men allowed the feud to continue, and I did love Charles, very much indeed.

A sudden creak on the floorboards outside my room made me stir. I leaned up on one elbow and listened. The room was eery in its darkness, and then I heard the faint click as my door handle was turned.

Quickly I lay down, hiding myself beneath the sheets, feigning sleep, yet straining to catch every sound. The door opening—someone creeping—closer, stealthily, until I could feel the warm breath of someone bending over me.

# *Nine*

THERE WAS NO MISTAKING the foul, liquor-smelling breath of my brother-in-law.

I managed to keep still, breathing evenly as if I was asleep, hoping that he would think so.

At last I sensed that he had moved away, so I opened my eyes for a second. A faint light reflected across the room from a candle and I could hear him at the fireplace.

My boots! He was looking at my boots to see if they were wet.

I felt my heart-beats quicken, and I grew numb with the cold sweat of fear. At any moment he would drag me from my bed, I was sure. He must have seen me ahead of him on the beach, and what reason would I have for a midnight walk in the middle of winter, except to spy on him?

Breathlessly, I listened as each boot was replaced in the hearth. Anxiously I waited!

Then once more I heard the click of the door handle. I opened my eyes and found myself enveloped in darkness again. I was too frightened to move. He might return. The soles of my boots must surely be wet from the frost-covered meadows. Sleep eluded me, so when I felt sure that the house was quiet again I lit my candle and got out of bed.

The fire was completely out now, not even one red ember left. I picked up my boots and found to my astonishment that they were quite dry and clean!

Had there really been enough warmth in the room to dry them, or was it my ghost safeguarding me again?

Or could I have been dreaming, after all? But the night's events were too definite. I *had* been on that walk with the monk—I knew I had.

Going to the window I drew back the heavy curtains and listened, as I so often did, to the sea, and the rattle of the pebbles on the shore. The moon was hidden and I stood watching the gathering grey clouds until the moon came out again and there, on the horizon, moving slowly at first but speeding up as the wind billowed out each sail, was the vessel I had seen earlier, anchored in the bay.

This was all the confirmation I needed that I had not been dreaming.

It was a gracious spectacle as the vessel headed for the open sea in full sail, the strong wind behind it soon taking it out of sight.

Sleep was fitful, partly because I had so much on my mind and partly because I was anxious not to oversleep. Greville was suspicious of me now, so I must take care to continue living as normally as possible.

He seemed to spend the next couple of days in the house more than usual, probably due to the fact that the weather was bitterly cold and the thick cotton-wool sky promised snow, which sure enough began to fall late one afternoon.

With Christmas only two weeks away the men on the estate had brought greenery to the house, so Emma and I spent the evening decorating the hall while Greville hung paper-chains, holly and mistletoe.

I was glad that the weather gave me an excuse for not visiting Hannah again, in answer to Emma's curiosity. I did try not to show my depression too much, though my heart was heavy at the loss of such a friendship, and I knew that eventually Emma would have to know, especially when I announced that I should not be accompanying them to church.

For the time being I managed to skilfully conceal the rift, but my thoughts were constantly at Lyme Towers, and Charles's gentle voice tortured my confused brain, but always Hannah's dove-grey eyes would intervene and spoil my memories.

What plans would they be making now? I wondered. How was the work progressing at the big house and even if they discovered old documents how could it help anyone now? And what if they proved that Greville was responsible for Edward's death? Would Charles have him thrown in prison?

The thought made my blood run cold. I couldn't stand by and see my sister have to bear such consequences: Charles couldn't be so cruel. But why shouldn't he be, I argued, if Greville was the brutal murderer, and all for a few pieces of paper, why shouldn't Charles bring him to justice?

Emma and Greville were happy now, happier than I had seen them for some time. It hardly seemed credible that Greville was the same person who had bullied the grovelling Job down on the beach. Truly Greville seemed to be a man of dual personality.

Next morning I woke to sunshine, and looking out of the window could see that already some of the light layer of snow was beginning to melt away.

Everywhere looked so picturesque, the crisp fresh air so inviting that I knew I wasn't going to spend another day cooped up in the house.

'Abbey! You must be out of your mind!' Emma reproved, as we met in the hall. 'Just because the sun is out does not mean that spring is here.'

I laughed at my sister.

'You know how I hate being indoors for long,' I

told her. 'I'm warmly dressed, and my boots are quite weatherproof. It's fun to walk in the snow. I shall go along the beach to the west, and up through the woods to the village. Is there anything you want?'

'No. I have already sent Lucy to do my shopping. If you had said at breakfast that you needed things from the village she could have saved you a journey.'

I laughed again.

'But I *want* to go out, Emma. I shall enjoy it.'

It was quite inexplicable why I felt so light-hearted as I set off down the lane, or why the mere thought of being in the great outdoors exhilarated me so much, and I smiled to myself as I thought of Emma's hopeless expression of disapproval.

Here and there I found the lane quite slippery, and the shingle beach too, so my pace was not up to its usual speed.

One or two of the local fisherman were hacking the ice from their upturned boats, but soon I was alone, glad to be free to enjoy the weak sun, glad to be going in the opposite direction to that which I had taken with the ghostly monk. I was trying hard to forget all about smuggling and feuds, even Edward's death.

The beach widened and the cliff was less steep than on the east side of Castle Grange.

As I walked I occasionally threw a piece of crust to a lonely seagull, and I became so absorbed in my private thoughts that I had walked a long way, and started as a strange voice came from the bushes.

'Good day.'

I must have looked quite frightened, for the old man, sitting on a huge boulder outside a tumbledown shack, spoke again.

'I'm sorry if I frightened you, missie. 'Tisn't often anyone comes by this far. Bleak and uninteresting, I s'pose.'

My smile was one of faint relief.

'How do you do,' I said. 'You gave me quite a start. I didn't expect to find anyone along here.' I glanced curiously at the wooden shack. 'You live . . . ?'

The old man, dressed in what appeared to be tattered Army clothes, looked strange, with snow-white hair showing beneath his shabby old hat, and a long beard, yet he was alert, his dark eyes friendly as he nodded in reply.

'But surely you find it very cold so near the sea?'

'Mm. 'Tis cold this time o' the year, but mostly the air in this part of Devon is warm. Sit ye down, missy, if you've a mind to. 'Tisn't often I gets company. And where might you be from then?'

There seemed to be one or two suitable rocks close by, and once I had taken the weight from my feet I realised how tired I was.

'I'm staying at Castle Grange,' I told the old man. 'Normally I live in Hampshire with my parents, but my sister has just had her first child so I'm staying for a while to lend a hand.'

'Then what brings you walking this way, miss?'

I smiled and looked out to the horizon.

'Perhaps I should have been a boy and become a sailor. I love the sea—and the country as well—just being out in the open air and I'm easily satisfied.'

The old man leaned forward on his stick and gazed at me.

'Yes, you are at home in these parts and I'm sure Devon is proud to offer hospitality to a fine young lady such as yourself. 'Tis my belief you'll find much happiness in the near future, miss.'

I looked at the old man suspiciously. What sort of tramp or beggar was he? The next question would surely be for my purse in payment for his fortune-telling.

'But not while you're staying at Castle Grange, I fear,' he went on speculatively.

'Please . . .' I begged. 'I don't wish to hear your fortune-telling. I'd rather take life as it comes.'

'Very wise, my dear, very wise,' he answered softly.

There was an awkward pause and something about the poor, harmless old creature made me feel sorry.

'Have you always lived in these parts?' I asked.

'Round about, missie, here and there.'

'Then you know the local families, and will know of my sister's husband's family—the Bonds?'

'Ah, ah!' He nodded his head remembering. 'I know the Bonds well enough.'

I grasped this opportunity to hear some local gossip.

'And the McClures too?' I ventured.

The old man's look had an understanding warmth about it, and I wondered if I had sounded too obvious in my interest.

'Sure enough,' he said, with a smile. 'A fine family, the McClures.'

The closer I looked into the old man's face the older he appeared to be, the skin was very wrinkled, his eyebrows bushy and white.

'I'm the oldest fisherman in Castle Rock, missie. There's been many a tale about the goings-on hereabouts in bygone days.'

'Please, tell me then,' I said earnestly. 'I like hearing about the old days. Have you ever seen the ghost, dressed like a monk?'

'So you've heard about him, have you?'

'Yes, yes,' I urged. 'Do you know the true story concerning him, and who he was?'

'I do indeed, my dear young lady, though it all happened a long time ago. His name was Francis Drummond, only son of Agnes Drummond.'

'And who exactly was Agnes Drummond?'

'A young kitchen maid. A right pretty young kitchen maid. Not a man who didn't have his eye set on her, there wasn't, so they do say.'

'But who did she marry in the end?' I asked with a merry laugh.

The old man's expression changed to one of solemnity, and I realised the story was not a happy one.

'She couldn't marry, missie. You see, 'twere one of the gentry folk from one of the big houses.'

'Oh dear,' I blundered. 'So did she go home to her family?'

'She had no family,' the old man said, quietly. 'Quite alone in the world she was, so the man responsible gave her that old house in the valley.'

'Of course, the ruins. Agnes Drummond took her own life there, and the son became a monk and made the house into a monastery.'

'So you know the story?'

'Not all of it, I think. Do go on. Did she live there alone with her son?'

'That's right, missie, and when he learned of his illegitimacy he was ashamed, and said he would go away into a monastery.'

I looked back along the shore, only just able to make out the archway of rock over the shore far away in the distance, and thought about my friend, the monk. It seemed characteristic of him to bear the shame of his mother's guilt.

'His mother loved the boy too much, they had lived too close, like hermits almost, and she couldn't bear to part with him. So she did away with herself. Afterwards the young man turned the house into a monastery, but there was a terrible storm several years later and the sea roared in and the cliff went crashing down into it, and all were drowned, even the monks who were having their supper.'

The old man's voice deepened, taking on a younger man's tone as he told the story so convincingly. Now he hung his head in silence, while I matched his story with the one I had read in the book.

'And now no one knows to whom the land belongs, or who the father of Francis Drummond was?' I mused.

'That, my dear, is what the feud is all about. The Bonds claimed that the man concerned was a Bond. The McClures disputed their story and said that the land was theirs, though no McClure ever admitted to being the father of Francis Drummond. Proud family, but just.'

'And no papers, deeds or wills left to settle the matter?' I asked.

'No—nothing that's yet come to light.'

I looked quickly at the old man.

'You believe there are still some in existence?'

The old man's gaze had come to rest on the rocks and headland far away.

'For the right person to discover, missie—maybe.'

His voice could only just be heard, he sighed and looked terribly old and weary.

'I'm most awfully sorry,' I said, apologetically. 'I've tired you—please forgive me for asking so many questions, but I have enjoyed talking with you. Is there anything I can do?'

He waved me aside with a long, bony hand.

'Bless you, child. I must go to my rest now.' He struggled to his feet and disappeared into the shack.

As soon as I found a pathway I left the beach, throwing the remains of the crusts Maud had given me to the seagulls, and walked thoughtfully towards the woods.

The squirrels were enjoying the sunshine, chasing

one another up and down the tall trees, and a family of robins caught my attention, and I wished I still had some bread for them. The snow lay quite thickly in places where the sun could not penetrate the trees, but I was grateful for the peacefulness to ponder over the old man on the beach.

At first I didn't take any notice of the soft thud, thud vibrating on the ground in the distance, but as the sound grew louder I realised a horseman was somewhere in the woods.

I kept on walking, but the rider was coming my way and I remembered Charles McClure's warning that it was not usual for a young lady to go out walking alone.

There was no definite pathway through the woods, so I hurried to where I could see a huge old oak tree and gathering my cloak round my skirts tightly I hid, and waited for the rider to pass by.

The soft thud drew nearer and I just prayed that he would turn off in another direction.

The tree creaked, and the frozen snow on its upper branches crackled as it began to melt and fall to the ground.

But the horse was slowing up, and still coming towards me. For a wild moment I wondered if I should run, but then I remembered Edward's fate, and stayed huddled where I was.

Now he was close behind the tree, and the slow thud eventually stopped.

I glanced cautiously this way, then the other, and I saw a huge black horse's head slowly appearing round the tree! I held my breath with fear as the rider jumped down and trapped me against the tree-trunk.

'Abbey, my dearest Abbey!'

I fell against my beloved Charles and sobbed hysterically.

'Abbey, please, I cannot bear to see you upset, please forgive me if you can.' I felt the warmth of his lips upon my brow.

Charles,' I whispered. 'I was so afraid. I did not think it would be you.'

'Who would go walking in the winter but you, dearest Abbey, and who else would pursue you but me? Once I spotted those dainty footprints in the snow I had no difficulty in following you. My only fear was that the snow would melt away before I found you. Hannah will be delighted, she was very angry with me.'

A smile crossed my face at the absurdity of Hannah being cross with Charles.

He lifted my chin and his expression was perplexed. 'Why do you smile, Abbey?'

'Hannah, cross with *you,* Charles—that could never be,' I said. 'In any case I should not have been so arrogant the other day, I am truly sorry.'

'You were distressed, my dear, and rightly so. As Hannah said, I should never have asked such a thing of you. She instructed me to find you, and make amends at all costs. But why could Hannah never be angry with me, Abbey?'

I looked up into Charles's face diffidently. What was in my mind had to be said. I could suppress my thoughts no longer.

'Hannah adores you far too much to allow herself to be displeased with you, Charles,' I said, softly.

His dark eyes penetrated mine. Then with a sigh he bent his head forward on his arm resting on the tree-trunk.

'I'm sorry, Charles, but it's no use trying to hide the fact that Hannah loves you very much indeed.'

'But Abbey, what strange notions have you been torturing yourself with? Hannah knows that I do not feel the same towards her. Oh, indeed I am very fond of her. Our friendship has been a lasting and happy one, but, my dear Abbey, I knew from the moment I saw you on the bridge . . .' He paused, and with a tender smile cupped my face in his hand. 'You, the brave outdoor girl, terrified by the silliest and most docile of my livestock, Humphrey—I knew that you were mine.'

'Charles!' I began, unable to believe this open declaration.

'And I thought you were beginning to love me in return,' he whispered.

'But I do—I do!' I cried, clinging to him for fear he would suddenly vanish. 'I do love you, Charles, more than I ever thought possible, but I believed that you and Hannah . . . ?'

'Shame on you, Abbey. That I should stoop to taking another man's wife?'

'But now that Edward is . . . ?'

'Edward was my friend, and I am very fond of Hannah, perhaps more with pity than with love. Her life with Edward was not easy—but then she is a strong-willed woman and not as warm-hearted as *my* woman must be. I have only seen Hannah cry once, and that was after you left Lyme Towers.'

'Oh, Charles, how I must have grieved her!'

'It was I who was at fault, my dearest, with my blundering suggestions. But, you see, I love you so much, and yet so long as the two families are at loggerheads how can I ask for your hand in marriage?'

'Charles, dear Charles. I too wish there could be an end to all the misunderstandings. I know now that Grenville is capable of many treacherous things.'

'He is still your brother-in-law, Abbey.'

'I have never liked him, Charles. There are times when he is good and kind, but mostly everyone is afraid of him. Charles, the other night after I had left Lyme Towers so rudely I was terribly confused and I sat thinking until midnight, and then . . .'

'And then?'

'The monk came for me.'

'The monk came for you! Abbey, what are you saying?' He laughed as if he thought I was talking nonsense.

'Charles, don't laugh, please. It's true, it must be the ghost of Francis Drummond that has visited me several times now. At first I was fascinated, but now I'm frightened. He calls me by name, and took me along the beach where I hid and watched Greville and his men bring contraband goods ashore from a vessel in the bay. But the ghost, Charles, the voice, I thought it was you at first.'

Charles kissed me tenderly.

'Dearest Abbey, can I believe that you love me so much that each voice reminds you of me—you flatter me, my dear, and I am so unworthy of such a true love.'

'Have you ever seen the ghost, Charles?'

'Yes—he calls me too, Abbey, but I do not answer. A man should not believe in ghosts.'

'But, Charles, I can only believe that in some way he is trying to help.'

'Help, yes, that I do need. I hope together we can prove what is right once and for all. If only Edward had left those papers in Hannah's safe keeping, or even at Lyme Towers.'

'Do you really think Greville has them?'

Charles nodded dismally. 'He did have them—though by now he has probably destroyed the evidence.'

'I will have a look at Castle Grange, just in case—if you think it will help?'

'No, Abbey, it might be best to leave things as they are. It is a deceitful thing to ask a woman to do.'

'But Greville is guilty of a serious crime as well as deceit,' I decreed. 'There is a small room off the library which I believe he uses as an office. When he is out I will see if I can find anything, there's just a chance that he might not have destroyed the papers—he is so full of cunning that there's no telling what he's up to.'

'You must use your own discretion, Abbey dear, but, please, take care, don't run unnecessary risks. If he so much as hurts a hair on your head, I will . . .'

'I can take care of myself, Charles. I fear always for Emma's sake, though, and must not do anything to jeopardise her and Louise. But the monk makes me feel I have some duty to perform here. Why, even the old fisherman told me I should find happiness soon—but not at Castle Grange.' I laughed as Charles held me close.

'What old fisherman, Abbey?'

'A very old man, with white hair and a long beard, but he seemed a wise old man and knew all about the feud. It started, he said, because Francis Drummond was illegitimate. Agnes Drummond was only a kitchen maid, and the father is unknown.'

'Who is this fisherman, Abbey, and where does he live? Perhaps it would help me to talk with him. I thought I knew all the locals.'

'He has an old shack on the beach.'

'But, Abbey . . .' Charles looked at me with scepticism. 'There are no shacks down on the beach.'

'Charles, dear, I am not stupid. I saw it and talked with the old man.'

'Come, let us get through the woods to the cliff edge, and you can show me.'

We were almost at the edge of the woods and together rode on Duke to the top of the cliff.

We stood holding hands looking back along the deserted beach.

'See, Abbey, there is no shack or fisherman there!'

# Ten

I SCANNED EVERY INCH of the shingle beach below, hanging perilously over the edge to see as close to the bushes as I could.

'Charles, I *know* he was there,' I said, hotly.

'My darling, you've been dreaming. There's no fisherman or shack down there,' he said, holding me tightly as I continued searching unsuccessfully.

'I *know* he was there,' I argued again. 'I thought I might have been dreaming the other night, but later looked out of my window and saw the vessel set sail and move out of sight. In any case, the fisherman told me about the ruins of the monastery, and also that Francis Drummond was illegitimate, which is something I hadn't heard before. The book doesn't mention that.'

'Which book is that?' Charles asked, pulling me away from the cliff edge and holding me close to him.

'A book which I found . . .' I stopped, and laughed, 'or rather the book found me when I was searching in the library at Castle Grange. That was my second encounter with the monk. I was anxious to read about the local history to try and trace whether anyone else had seen a ghost in these parts when the candle suddenly went out, and during a fierce draught I had a fleeting glimpse of the monk again. Afterwards, I found this book at my feet.'

'Do you still have the book?'

'Yes, Charles. *The Receding Coast of Devon* is its

title, and I've kept it hidden in my room owing to the strange way in which it appeared. I'll let you see it, I think you may find it interesting.'

'I'll look in the library at Lyme Towers and see if we have a copy. But that still doesn't solve the mystery of the fisherman. You have seen for yourself that the beach is quite deserted.'

'I shall walk again along the beach until I find him,' I said, defiantly.

Suddenly, Duke, who was grazing nearby, whinnied, and reared up. Charles and I both looked, and just for a brief second saw a figure standing among the trees.

I felt Charles's fingers tighten on my arm, but instinctively I pulled away from him and ran towards the figure.

But the old fisherman had disappeared again!

Frantically I searched among the bushes, but there was no one there, and when I joined Charles again he had turned quite pale as he pacified Duke.

'Charles, you did see him then, didn't you?'

He held out his arms to me and I went anxiously to him.

'Yes, Abbey. I saw—someone. An old man with a beard— and then he was gone. It's quite uncanny, but I'm beginning to believe in your ghost, fisherman, or monk.'

'But why should he visit me, Charles? I'm neither Bond nor McClure,' I asked, glad of the comfort of his cheek against mine.

Now he held me at arm's length and looked deep into my eyes.

'Perhaps that's it, Abbey. You are destined to become a McClure. Say you'll marry me as soon as things are settled?'

He hugged me to him and I closed my eyes contentedly, hardly daring to believe that we were together. His clothes smelled earthy, a healthy outdoor smell, and I felt secure at last.

'Oh, Charles, I am *so* happy—of course I want to marry you.'

'You must be tired, Abbey, you've walked a long way this morning. Look, there's a broken tree trunk, come and sit down with me, there is so much we have to talk about. I have a great deal of work before me, Abbey, and not all concerned with settling the land dispute with your brother-in-law.'

'Hannah told me she was helping you at Lyme Towers—to do with your estate.'

'Yes, that's right. Another of Hannah's merits is that she is an excellent business woman. Edward was good, but shied a little from hard work, whereas Hannah will stick to it for hours, and seems to revel in it. I am considering making her my secretary—with your approval, of course.'

'Anything you want, Charles,' I readily agreed. 'I shall look forward to seeing Hannah again very soon, if she doesn't think too badly of me.'

'I told you, she ordered me out to find you. We guessed nothing would keep you indoors once the sun came out. Little did I think you'd be taking midnight walks along the beach, though, and all by yourself. You must take more care, Abbey.'

'But I was not alone, Charles. The ghost took great care of me—but why should he now change into a fisherman—or is it another ghost, do you suppose? I do hope they are not on opposing sides!'

We laughed happily together.

'Now you really are letting your imagination run away with you. I only wish that you were not in any way involved, my dear Abbey, but if we are to be married—oh, if only I had those papers!'

'I will search Castle Grange at every opportunity, Charles, or could I ask Greville outright? I am not afraid of him—but no, I must consider Emma, and Louise.'

'Do be very careful. I fear we may have lost all claim, though, if we cannot find further evidence.'

'Wait a minute,' I said, excitedly. 'What was it the fisherman said? I asked him if there were any deeds or wills, and he replied: "Maybe—for the right person to find." If only he had given me a clue.'

'If only,' Charles echoed. 'Yes, I am convinced that my work must be to that end, and am anxious to see the whole matter cleared up once and for all. When I came home to be at my father's bedside I was appalled at the poverty among the local countryfolk. Much as I would have liked to continue my military career I felt my duty lay here in Castle Rock, to try to improve the living conditions of the workers on the estate.'

'But that is a great task, Charles.'

He sighed. 'It would have been a good thing if your brother-in-law would have joined forces with me in the cause for the repeal of the Corn Laws. It isn't right that the bread we produce is such an enormous price that only the rich can afford to buy, while our workers and their families starve. These heavy taxes must be cut.'

I could only gaze admiringly at the man I loved, and longed to be of some help in achieving his ambition.

'We are on the threshold of a great age, Abbey,' he he went on. 'A new era, a revolutionary era, under a lively young Queen, which will see many changes in industry as well as in agriculture. I have travelled extensively and seen squalor, and much undeserved cruelty. I want to see better living conditions in my country, even though I have little enough funds with which to fight. I should like to see Castle Rock become a united community, all working for the benefit of each other.'

'You have high ideals, Charles, too high, I fear, for men like Greville Bond. He only works and plunders for himself.'

'But your sister loves him.'

'Indeed, yes. They are devoted to all outward appearances, but I fancy Emma is rather afraid of her husband.'

'That shouldn't be,' Charles said, taking both my hands in his. 'I hope I shall never give you cause for such fear, my darling.'

'I know you will not, Charles, for you are of quite a different character.'

'Marriage must be by mutual consent. It must be a partnership. I hope you agree, Abbey? I do not hold with arranged marriages, and our children must be allowed to choose for themselves, and never forced to marry against their wishes.'

'I do so agree with you, Charles. Why else would I have come to Castle Grange?'

'Dearest Abbey.' He pressed his lips to mine and the strength of his body intensified my rapture. 'If only we could be married tomorrow—even today.'

'I would marry you right now if that's what you wanted,' I told him, softly.

'Oh, Abbey, my dear, how can that be? I could not go to your father and ask your hand knowing that I should be splitting two devoted sisters apart. You realise that's what it would mean, surely?'

I clung to him and sighed deeply.

'Yes, I suppose Greville would oppose us with compelling force.'

'I do not wish to see you banished by your own

family. We must strive to end the dispute as soon as possible, so that when we marry our wedding will be a splendid occasion, a family occasion to give us the right start to a happy marriage.'

For the next few minutes the world stood still as we avowed our love for one another. . . .

'Charles, I must go. It must be past time for luncheon, and I was supposed to be going to the village.'

'I am sad to let you go at all, dearest. Can I take you to the village and then back to Castle Grange?'

'Better not,' I decided. 'I will return and say nothing of my meeting with the fisherman, or you. Tomorrow afternoon Emma and I are to go to see the Misses Bell to have our gowns fitted. They are a present from Greville for Christmas, though I am not too happy about the matter, for I am convinced the cloth is some of his contraband goods. Perhaps I will visit Hannah afterwards.'

'I shall tell her to expect you for tea, then. It might be better, in the circumstances, to go to the cottage, though, of course,' he whispered intimately, 'she will prepare for three.'

His teasing smile was exciting, his lips sensuous on mine as we said goodbye.

No longer did I feel tired, and my feet skimmed the snow-spangled meadows and lanes with a new purpose as I made my way home to Castle Grange.

My heart was full to overflowing with love for Charles, if only I could sing it out to the world, but it had to be a secret. Could I whisper it to Emma? I wondered. No, not yet. The time was not right. I must do nothing to come between husband and wife.

I put my head round the dining room door before going up to my room.

'I'm sorry if I'm late, Emma. It was so lovely out I just kept walking.'

Greville was sitting opposite Emma at the table, his back to the door.

'I'm about to serve, Abbey, so you're just in time, Emma said, without glancing my way.

'I'll take my cloak upstairs,' I called, and bounded up the oak staircase, my skirts held high.

How could I contain myself? My elation must be obvious I knew by just one glance in the mirror.

I tore at my bonnet ribbons and after discarding cloak and shawl splashed my flushed cheeks with soft rain water from the china jug in an effort to control my excitement before meeting Emma and Greville.

Perhaps it was only my imagination, after all, or perhaps they were too preoccupied to notice my high spirits, for neither made any comment.

The next day was milder and the remainder of the snow quickly disappeared.

'I shall visit Hannah after we have finished at the drapery store,' I told Emma after luncheon.

'Oh!' She sounded surprised. 'As you didn't come to church with me last Sunday, and have not been to the cottage lately, I thought you had at last come to your senses, Abbey.'

'Wha do you mean, Emma, come to my senses?'

'You cannot be so stupid, Abbey, that you do not understand that one day Hannah Lacey will become Mrs. McClure?'

I lowered my gaze as I pulled my gloves on fiercely.

'I have seen no evidence to suggest that that is the case,' I said, quietly.

'Half the village is gossiping. She practically lives at Lyme Towers,' Emma retorted.

'I told you, Emma, she is helping Charles.'

'Ugh! How easily they pull the wool over your eyes,

Abbey. But *I* cannot be your keeper. I have warned you and if you will pay no heed . . .' She let out an impatient sigh. 'Come along, we shall be late for our appointment. Miss Bell would prefer us to have our fittings while the shop is closed for dinner.'

Even in the carriage I was obliged to keep my face half hidden by my cloak collar lest Emma should wonder at my unashamed smile.

Dear Emma, how disillusioned she was, to be sure. What reprimands there would be if she had but caught a glimpse of me in Charles's arms but twenty-four hours since, and now I would soon be in his arms again . . .

I took little interest in my gown save to suggest that the waist be made a little tighter. After all, I must consider my fashion a little more than usual, as I wanted to look my best for Charles.

Emma fussed, and frequently changed her mind regarding the style of her gown, but I envied her her beauty, for whatever the colour or design she would look enchanting.

At last the carriage drew up outside the cottage and I stood at the gate and watched Emma depart.

Only then did the door open and Hannah and I embraced each other, unable to speak for tears of joy.

Afterwards we sat and talked, trying unsuccessfully to unravel the mysteries of the past, but very soon we were interrupted as the clatter of horses' hooves heralded the arrival of Charles.

He made no apology to Hannah as he held me very tightly, kissing every inch of my radiant face. I tried to remonstrate with him, but soon realised that Hannah had discreetly left the room.

'Abbey, relax. Hannah knows our feelings, she understands,' he whispered.

'But it must be awful for her to see me in the arms of the man she loves.'

'Hannah has loved me silently for many years. If I am happy, then she is too. I have never given her any encouragement; it would have been wrong to give her false hope. I think I know Hannah better than she knows herself. In time you will come to love and accept her as she is, dearest.'

'But I love her very much,' I told Charles, quickly. 'Only when we met again today did I realise just how much I value her friendship.' I looked up into his dark eyes. He smiled into mine, holding my chin gently in his strong hand.

'I do declare your eyes are almost blue, Abbey. When we first met I thought they were green. There have been times when I have likened them to Hannah's grey ones, too.' He kissed my forehead lightly. 'I do believe you're a witch,' he teased softly.

'Just because my eyes change colour?' I laughed back. 'At home I am constantly reminded that my eyes are—well, not quite nice in some ways. Mother says they reveal my mood too well, and show a shrewdness not complimentary in a young lady.'

'I think they show your true character, my darling. A delightful intelligence which I find much more attractive than eyes which demonstrate no emotion. It might also be amusing to be warned of your mood. I can then be about my estate affairs before you hurl the china at me.'

'Charles!' I remonstrated. 'You sound as if you anticipate a nagging wife.'

'I will not allow you to become that. Indeed, I shall see that you never change.'

His lips were fierce with passion on mine, and I wished that I could hold on to that moment for ever, but a light tap on the door warned us of Hannah's return, though Charles would not release me immediately.

The lingering tender smile told me so much more than words about the man who had captured my heart.

He turned to Hannah.

'Don't do that again, Mrs. Lacey,' he said, with a glint of amusement in his expression.

'I'm sorry, Charles,' Hannah said with a worried frown. 'What did I do?'

'Knock on your own door. We cannot hide our feelings any longer, Hannah dear, and we are both grateful that we can meet in your home, but it is *your* home, and we shall honour that.'

'You know I am delighted to act as Abbey's chaperone, and I want you to meet here as often as you like until things are a little more settled. I promise not to make my presence too obvious.' She laughed vivaciously, and I understood for myself that she only cared for Charles's happiness, and asked for little else in life.

'Charles,' she continued. 'You mentioned taking Abbey round the estate. I don't wish to hurry you, but dusk falls so early in December.'

'Of course, Hannah, thank you for reminding me. When I do manage to have Abbey all to myself I get carried away.' He pulled me yet closer to him, his hand firm and possessive around my waist. 'I've brought a young filly over with me, so that we can ride together if you would care to, Abbey? I am anxious that you should see the extent of my estate and riding will be less tiring for you, although I know you prefer to walk. Silver Quest is still a bit frisky, but I think you'll be able to handle her. She does behave quite well when riding beside Duke.'

'Silver Quest,' I repeated. 'What a charming name? I'm sure she will carry me well, Charles.'

'If she suits you, my dear, she is yours, a present from me. I was home on leave eighteen months ago when she was foaled, and somehow she marked the beginning of changes in my life. I knew at that time that Father would not last long, and although he never tried to press me into returning to Lyme Towers for good, I felt it was fairly evident that that was his last remaining hope. The mare's name is Silver Star, so I decided the offspring should be Silver Quest to remind me of my new quest to reinstate Lyme Towers.'

'You're quite a sentimentalist, Charles,' I told him, squeezing his hand.

'Indeed I am, and proud of it. Many a McClure before me has been too. Many a strange deed has been performed in the name of sentimentalism.'

'Be off with you,' Hannah chided at his foolishness. 'And while you are gone I shall prepare tea.'

Silver Quest was a small mare, unusually marked for a dapple-grey, with an elegant long white nose. We quickly made friends, and although I sensed a reckless streak in her, one word from Charles and she was instantly obedient.

We cantered across the meadows and through the woods while Charles pointed out the boundaries of his vast estate.

Then, as we came to a steep riding track, he held my reins as well as his own.

'I can't have Silver Quest getting too frisky and making off with you here,' he said. 'It gets wet and slippery as the rocks get larger.'

'Are we near the sea then?' I asked, though it did not appear so, as the trees met overhead and the track was narrow.

'Quite near. I fancy you have not ventured this far yet, even though your adventurous heart has been more than a little curious about the place.'

Cautiously we went down the perilous slope and then I could hear the rush of water. After several minutes the track opened out into a clearing and after dismounting Charles tethered the horses to a tree, and we went on foot through the trees where Charles showed me the natural waterfall.

Sparkling ice-cold water cascaded down the rocky gorge, and then as if the devil himself was in pursuit it plunged noisily over the huge rocks into a wide gully.

'Here the stream goes out to meet the sea,' Charles told me. 'Let me hold you now, Abbey, as we must walk over the rocks to the cave.'

With Charles holding my hand tightly I placed my feet where he told me. The rocks at the side of the gully rose higher, and then the path became wider as we came to flatter ground.

'Now we are safe enough,' he said. 'Look, here is the Devil's Arch—and there is the remainder of the cave.'

Charles pointed to the left-hand side of the arch of rock under which we were now standing.

'There was once a huge cave there, where pirates lived—but that was many years ago, even before the storm took the monastery out to sea.'

'So we are at the ruins?' I cried excitedly.

'Just a section of it, and this is one way to reach it, though dangerous. I brought you here to show you the natural beauty of the waterfall, *and* to warn you, young lady, *not* to try exploring here on your own. The cave entrance is sealed off with rock for safety because it is now under several feet of water. But look beyond the arch—another world.' He guided me through the dark sombre rocks and I could see daylight ahead, and then we stood out in an open space, wet and muddy underfoot with a small building in the centre.

'The Monk's Chapel,' Charles said, 'or what is left of it.'

He took my hand in his again as we entered the tiny building, barely four walls and only half a roof now, and solemnly we stood before what was once the altar, above which remained the stained-glass window, depicting the twelve apostles, facing westwards, still intact.

'It's quite beautiful,' I said, 'and how amazing that it is still almost undamaged.'

'It is believed to have been made entirely by the monks themselves, and disastrous to think that there is no history obtainable relating to this place, prior to the storm.'

'How peaceful it is here, Charles,' I whispered. 'One can almost imagine the monks singing Evensong.'

He held me close and kissed me gently.

'Come and see the ruins, my darling, you are getting too serious.'

We crossed the open space, where, as the ground sloped downwards again, bushes and trees thickened, and looking up towards the headland on our right I saw the crumbling stone wall where I had been caught in the storm on the day when I had first met Charles.

It was barely three months ago, yet seemed like only yesterday, and so much had happened since. Emma had had her first baby, Louise Victoria; Edward had been killed, and I had fallen in love with Charles.

Deep down inside me I was happier than I had ever been in my life before, but there was this depressing cloud overshadowing our happiness, a dark forbidding cloud which made me afraid of being too happy. But Charles did not know the reason for my silence as we wound our way through the thickets, and then suddenly we were there!

A mass of stonework and rubble. Here and there parts of walls remained standing with gaping holes where windows and doors had once been.

'I have not been here for some time, Abbey. It is even more ruined than I remember. I suppose every year the sea takes a little more,' Charles said, nostalgically.

At closer scrutiny I could see that only the outer walls on the one side remained, now partially covered with ivy and evergreens. We walked over heaps of rubble and masonry to what had been the interior. I suddenly felt cold and clutched at Charles's arm.

'What's the matter, my darling? I cannot believe you of all people are afraid,' he said.

'No, no, it's just that, well, the thought of all those monks being drowned. My monk—my ghost—it must have been awful, Charles.'

'Now who's a sentimentalist?' He smiled down at me reassuringly, but then grew serious. 'You're right—it must have been horrifying. No wonder Francis Drummond came back to haunt the place.'

'But he must have a reason, surely? Some unfinished business, perhaps?'

Charles shook his head. 'Who knows?'

We walked about trying to place the rooms of the old creeper-covered monastery, and then on the south side we came to where the windows had once overlooked the bay, but where now the sea had gained access. It lapped over the stonework and echoed eerily through the arches.

'When I was a little boy,' Charles told me, 'we used to play down there.'

'But that must have been very dangerous.'

'The water had not penetrated in so far then. Only

at very high tide and during a fierce storm did it cover the rocks and come through this far, just as on the night of the freak storm when most of the house went into the sea, taking the monks with it. I expect when the tide is well out you can still get down to the rooms on the floor below.'

I turned away, nauseated at the horror of what had taken place so many years ago.

Charles must have sensed my distress, for he said kindly:

'Go back to the chapel, Abbey, and then walk upwards towards the boundary wall. I'll go and fetch the horses, I shall be quicker alone, and it's not an easy path for you to tread. I shall be with you in no time.'

I was grateful for a few quiet moments to think during my slow walk to the wall, but no sooner had I reached it than I heard the horses approaching, and very soon I had remounted and we were heading back to the pond, and the bridge where Humphrey was awaiting us eagerly.

Reaching the green outside Hannah's cottage Charles helped me dismount.

'You look sad, Abbey,' he said, as he held me firmly round my waist. 'I thought you wanted to see the ruins?'

'I did, Charles, and thank you for taking me there. I must confess, though, I found it a melancholy place.'

Charles smiled as he released me.

'Then I shall have no fear that you will venture there alone. Go along into Hannah, my dear, I shall take the horses to the stables, and return with the carriage, ready for your return to Castle Grange.'

Sitting before the log fire, enjoying a reunion tête-à-tête, should have given me pleasure, but surrounded by uncertainty I could find no enthusiasm for gaiety.

At least I felt for the first time that I could relax with Charles and Hannah, and found some consolation in being able to talk freely about Edward's death, as well as disclosing what little I knew of Greville's movements. I was able to give my willing listeners a concise account of my night's escapade along the beach, and they in turn told me that they knew some of Greville's men passed through Charles's land at night, taking contraband spirits and wines up to the inn.

But after talking of little else for the best part of two hours we could find no immediate solution, and our future prospects looked grim. There could be no public engagement for us, no wedding plans yet, only clandestine meetings with Charles, through Hannah's kindness.

She allowed us a few moments alone before my departure, and not a second did we waste.

Nestling against Charles's strong frame I knew the magnitude of our love, and gained comfort from his tender assurance.

'It won't always be like this, my darling,' he whispered. 'We couldn't endure it, and I wouldn't expect such untiring patience from you. Will you give me a little more time—a few weeks perhaps? Then if there is no other way, I must go to your father.'

I sighed unhappily.

'Father will not hear a word against Greville. Not that he has that high an opinion of him, just that he it too weak to make a stand. Mother will be difficult and I am afraid our marriage will be marred from the start.'

Charles gently placed a finger over my lips.

'You are distraught, Abbey. Don't think about it yet. Just one clause on a piece of paper could give us the clue, and help us to end this ancient feud. Then nothing will stand in our way.'

'Greville will always stand in our way. He will fight us to the bitter end, Charles.'

'We must hope that we can appeal to the good in him when the time comes, for Emma's sake, and their children. I mean to do everything in my power to see that there is no feud for the next generation to inherit.'

'And I shall do all I can to help, Charles dear. The first thing I must do is to search Castle Grange from top to bottom for those papers.'

Charles laughed at my enthusiasm.

'It will be of little use, Abbey. If Greville took the papers from Edward's body he would surely have destroyed them by now. Please don't do anything to antagonise your brother-in-law.'

If only I had listened to those words!

So obsessed did I become with the belief that through Greville the dispute could be ended, and Charles and I could be married, that I became careless in my eagerness.

A few days elapsed before an opportunity arose, and when one evening Greville was absent from the house, and Emma retired early, I went to the library on the pretext of looking for a book to read.

Even the servants seemed to have retired early, the house seemed empty in its silence.

I tiptoed from the library into the small adjoining room Greville used as an office, and placed the candle on the table.

The neat orderliness of his books and papers surprised me. Even the drawers in the big oak table were tidy, and it made my task much simpler.

Surreptitiously I went through each drawer in turn, taking care to replace everything as I found it, but my search was fruitless.

A centre drawer was locked, which only added to my determination to see inside. I tugged and pulled, and finally set about it with a hairpin.

So absorbed was I that I heard no sound of anyone approaching until the sudden swish of the big brass rings on the heavy curtain in the corner interrupted my unsuccessful attempt at lock-picking.

Behind the curtain was a narrow open doorway, through which came my brother-in-law!

# *Eleven*

I WAS NOT THE SORT to get up and run. It would have been better if I had; instead I remained on my knees in front of the table. Casually I bent the hair-pin back into its proper shape and pushed it into my hair.

Greville showed no surprise at finding me there. Calmly he walked into the room, closing and locking the narrow door, which I had not noticed before, and drew the curtain over it again.

I backed slowly to the corner of the table. He, with no more than a couple of lengthy strides, reached the door to the library, closed and locked that as well, stuffing the keys into his waistcoat pocket.

Then he began walking towards me, a satisfied grin spreading across his ugly face.

'Well, Abbey, to what do I owe this not altogether unexpected pleasure? I anticipated such a visit, though before this.'

I found myself instinctively edging away from him, round the table. He kept on coming.

Self-confidently, I had told Charles I was not afraid of my brother-in-law, but now, with only a table between us in a small room from which there was no escape, I was not so sure.

'I——I want the papers you took from Edward's body,' I blurted, tossing my head in the air.

He blinked nervously. Had my honest admission unnerved him?

'You brazen hussy!' he growled. 'And what gives you the right to suggest I took them?'

'Who else would want them? In any case, the publican says you were the only man to leave the inn while Edward was there, so what other reason would you have for bribing him, to keep silent?'

I watched his eyes narrow as still we inched our way round the table.

'Greville,' I went on, in a softer tone, 'surely you must see this whole business is achieving nothing. Everyone knows that Edward was killed in an accident, no one could be so deliberately cruel, even the coroner said so. Why go on with this silly feud, over land which you know isn't yours?'

'Who says it's not mine, you meddling wench? It's the McClure's word against the Bond's, and has been for many a year, over a century in fact.

'And if the papers you found gave such evidence Charles would be the first to concede.'

He eyed me suspiciously, and kept coming after me.

' "Charles" now, is it?' he sneered.

Suddenly he threw himself across the corner of the table and grabbed my wrist.

Shrewd though I was, I had not foreseen this action.

In seconds the top of my gown was pulled off my shoulders as with savage passion Greville caught me in his arms, kissing my neck and face. I pushed and beat at him with my fists.

'Greville!' I cried. 'Please—what do you think you are doing? Have some consideration for Emma, I beg you. I am only a young innocent . . .'

He held me so close I could not breathe, but he stopped kissing me and looked down into my face, laughing.

'But not so innocent, I think, my dear Abbey, or what would a young innocent be doing in the arms of Charles McClure over in the meadows? Come on, Abbey, you're not so cold and hard as you try to make me believe.' He kissed me fiercely on my lips. 'Let me come to your room, and we'll say no more about this affair,' he whispered.

'Greville,' I pleaded earnestly. 'You must be drunk, you cannot know what you are saying. Have you no thought for your wife and little daughter?'

'I want a son, Abbey. You have all the makings of a strong woman who could bear me a son. It wouldn't be so awful—I can send Emma home to your parents. You're sisters after all.'

I couldn't stand his odious breath upon me, nor could I believe he knew what he was suggesting, but I had little enough strength to fight this giant of a man.

'Emma will bear you a son, Greville. You must be patient,' I gasped. 'Let me go, please, and *I'll* say nothing of this to anyone.'

He seemed to be losing control as he held me tighter to him, bending me backwards over the table, greedily tearing at my gown.

'I've got you now, my dear, just where I want you, and there's no point in your worrying your head over land, when there's more interesting things to do.'

'But I want to . . .'

His thick lips pressing into my mouth prevented me from continuing, so, panic-stricken, I bit with all my might.

He let me go at once, guarding his mouth with the back of his hand. I jumped to the floor and pulling my shawl closer round me darted across the room, putting the table between us again.

'You vicious little . . .' He broke off as if thinking twice before cursing me. My sharp-edged teeth had succeeded in breaking the skin, and as he removed his hand it had blood on it, and slowly the thick red liquid trickled down his chin.

'So you think I killed Edward Lacey? And you think I took some papers or other?' he said slowly, then let forth a hideous laugh as he unlocked and opened the door to the library. 'You're anxious to find them, no doubt, Miss Abigail, so go ahead and search—you've got a long night ahead of you,' and with a great shout of laughter he went out, locking the door behind him.

I ran to the door, pleading: 'Greville, no, please let me out—let me out!' But the heavy oak door imprisoned me and my voice.

It seemed as if I banged for hours before realising that no one would hear. I sat down on a straight-backed leather chair, exhausted.

The little room was cold and draughty so that the candle flickered and burnt down unevenly. I looked about for another, but it was obvious that I should soon be in total darkness, so making the most of the light whilst I still had some, I went across to the door behind the curtain. Presumably because of the curtain I had not seen the door on previous visits to the library. What lay behind it? I wondered. And to where did it lead?

I knelt down, holding the candle at every angle, desperately trying to peep through the keyhole, but could see only black emptiness.

Could I make my escape through the window? was my next thought, but looking about realised that there were only two long narrow windows, high up on the outside wall, which must be the reason for the little room always looking so dark.

Accepting the fact that I was doomed to spending the night here, I placed the candle back on the table and tried each of the three chairs in turn to find the most comfortable, then arranged my shawl around my shoulders and back to give me maximum warmth.

The candle flame died and flared alternately, and I was grateful for its company, but soon it died altogether and I was in darkness, alone with my thoughts.

Surely Greville would soon come to his senses and release me. I couldn't be kept locked up indefinitely, or Emma would become over-anxious.

All this, I thought, for a few papers which I was positive Greville had destroyed by now.

My future with Charles looked black, and after this incident with Greville I could not remain here under the same roof. And yet I could not tell Emma what had occurred either.

I would go home to my parents at the earliest opportunity, but as my weary brain tried to make preparations I remembered that my parents had gone to Brittany to stay with relatives for Christmas.

Drowsiness finally gave way to sleep, of a sort, but as I grew progressively colder I became wider awake.

My feet were numbed, so I groped cautiously round the table to where I had seen another chair, and dragged it back to where I had been sitting so that I could put my feet up. Through the long cold hours I either sat in the chair and dozed, or walked blindly round the table a few times to get warm again.

When dawn's first eery light peeped through the windows I concentrated on the welcome glow, and must have dropped off into a deep slumber, for suddenly I woke with a start!

Someone was standing in the library doorway!

I cannot tell who looked the most shocked—myself or Mrs. Thwaites.

She threw her hands in the air when I struggled to my feet, dropping her broom and bucket.

'Lawks a mercy!' she exclaimed. 'Why, Miss Abigail, what are you a doing of 'ere?'

It was still quite early and barely light, so that finding me locked in Greville's room gave Mrs. Thwaites a dreadful fright, but she quickly recovered and came closer.

'My dear child,' she said with alarm, 'you're frozen stiff.' She took my hands between hers and rubbed vigorously. 'How on earth did you get yourself locked in here?'

'I'd rather not go into that just now, Mrs. Thwaites,' I said. 'I'm so relieved to see you, now I can go to bed properly.'

'You'll take a chill and no mistake. 'Tisn't as if there's ever a fire going in the library. Come along, my dear, I'll help you to your room and have a good fire going there in no time.'

I indicated that I didn't wish to disturb the rest of the household, but as soon as we reached my room and closed the door, I poured out the whole sordid story to the housekeeper.

'Emma must never know, Mrs. Thwaites, but I cannot go near my brother-in-law again.'

'Now you must calm yourself, Miss Abigail, and while I go and get a hot drink and the warming pan, you get yourself undressed.'

I allowed myself to be fussed over, and although my limbs ached unbearably I began to revive. Mrs. Thwaites was worth her weight in gold, no sooner had I sipped the hot drink than a huge fire blazed and crackled cheerfully in the hearth.

'Don't you fret Miss Abigail,' she told me. 'A couple of days in bed will do you no harm. I'll tell Mrs. Bond that you've taken a chill, most likely 'flu, and it won't do for her to get near you because of infecting the baby. I'll attend to you myself—and I'll see that no one comes near.'

She was as good as her word, and watched over me loyally so that I could relax and sleep through most of the day. But as darkness descended again I became restless, and wondered if Greville would try to visit me.

'It's no good, Mrs. Thwaites, I cannot stay in this house. Mr. Bond must know that you found me in his office.'

'Mr. Bond knows that *I* know a thing or two, miss,' she said knowingly, 'and if I say you're not to be disturbed, he'll take heed. He's kept out of my way most of the day, so it isn't likely he'll come looking for trouble tonight. I shan't leave you, miss, I'll sleep in the chair by the fire, and if you feel like talking, well, I'm close by.'

'Oh, no, Mrs. Thwaites, you must go to your own room, and have your proper night's rest, it wouldn't be right . . .'

'Now don't take on, my dear. I've sat many a night with your sister.'

'With Emma?' I asked. 'But why?'

'The master has some queer ways at times, miss. A bit wild like, you see, and Mrs. Emma used to take fright at first.'

'I hope he's never harmed her. Why Emma should want to marry such a man I cannot think.'

Mrs. Thwaites laughed. 'She likes his manly ways, my dear, and he wouldn't hurt her, he thinks too much of her for that, but, you see, he gets boisterous like, with too much drink.'

'It's my belief that he drinks a great deal too much all the time,' I said, angrily.

Mrs. Thwaites sighed. 'Yes, like his father before

him—his smuggling won't ever make him a fortune. He drinks it all away his-self.'

'Thank goodness Charles doesn't indulge in such dangerous exploits,' I said.

Mrs. Thwaites looked across at me kindly.

'You'll have a good man there, Miss Abigail. He's had a sound training in the military. Mind you, folk in these parts don't take exception to a bit of smuggling. 'Tis what you might call their heritage. 'Tis always been done, you see, and, well, so long as no one gets hurt, where's the harm?'

'Yes, I suppose you're right, but the sooner I get away from Greville Bond and his smuggling the better. If only the dispute could be settled, though, before I go to my parents. I must get away, but where? There's no one at Sheridan Lodge—they've gone to Brittany.'

'Don't you think you should tell Mr. McClure what happened, miss? Or at least let him know you're not well.'

'Yes, I must write to Charles, but how will he get it?'

'I'll see to that. You write a letter and I'll get young Lucy to take it to the village. She'll be going home tomorrow and her brother will deliver it. He's been helping out at the McClure stables since Mr. Bond couldn't place him here.'

'Yes, I'll do that. Lucy is a sensible girl, and I hope will treat the matter in confidence. We don't want half the village knowing what happened.'

'She won't say anything, miss, 'cos she won't know anything. Best if you was to put your letter to Mr. McClure in with one for Mrs. Lacey, then I can tell Lucy to ask her brother to take it to Mrs. Lacey 'cos you've got a chill—and no one will be any the wiser.'

'That's a splendid idea, Mrs. Thwaites, but I don't

feel like writing just now, I'll do it first thing in the morning.'

I tried to settle down to sleep while Mrs. Thwaites stoked up the fire and prepared the big rocker with blankets for herself. Although I felt guilty at imposing upon her good nature, I was very relieved to know that I was not alone.

A little after midnight I woke with a stiff neck and sore throat, and became restless with a prolonged bout of coughing and persistent sneezing, but apart from feeling uncomfortably hot I didn't really feel ill.

Mrs. Thwaites was snoring loudly. The fire was well banked, now a bright orange and red glow. I didn't want my coughs and sneezes to wake her, so I slipped from the bed to get a drink of water.

Suddenly I wasn't sleepy any more and decided to sit by the fire and contemplate where I would go when I left Castle Grange.

My thoughts soon drifted to their usual course, and Charles. Yes, now was as good a time as any to write to him.

As I poured out my heart in the silence of the night I felt as if he were there with me, but pausing to read what I had written I knew that I was being careless. For Emma's sake I must not write about Greville's advances to me, even though it burdened me with distaste and I longed to talk things over with someone.

My next and even third attempts went into the fire, and I wached the pale blue vellum blacken and curl before disintegrating.

At last I compiled a simple note saying that I had been caught searching for the documents and that Greville had locked me in the room all night. Now I was in bed with a chill, but as soon as I was better I should be going away. I ended with an honest declaration of my love for him, telling him that I was only causing trouble by staying, even though I hated being parted from him. A short explanatory note to Hannah accompanied it, and after sealing the envelope addressed to Hannah I left it on the mantelpiece and returned to my bed.

Little had I thought that my stay with my sister would come to such an abrupt end. What was I going to tell Emma, I wondered, to explain my sudden departure? Perhaps I could let her think that Charles and I had quarrelled. But I didn't want anyone to think that. Nothing could be further from the truth. I wanted everyone to know how much I loved him, and could only long for the day when we could publicly announce our engagement.

Just to close my eyes and relive the cherished moments up on the meadow; and later riding Silver Quest at his side, visiting the ruins and feeling strangely moved at the way the sea had claimed the monastery, I needed little imagination to feel the warmth and strength of my Charles, and gradually I was soothed to sleep . . .

It was very late when I stirred and found Mrs. Thwaites attending to the fire. Almost as soon as I started talking to her the coughing began again. From then on I was given one remedy after another, and when Emma called to me from the passageway my voice convinced her that I really had got a chill.

I begged her not to stay near my room, even, lest she should carry the infection to the baby, so after assuring her that I had all that I required she went away.

Sleep carried me through most of that day. It was not possible to know which of Mrs. Thwaites' remedies cured me, but certainly by the following morning I was much better, so by midday decided to dress and sit by the fire.

Mrs. Thwaites constantly attended me, and during the afternoon we began to pack my belongings, though I still had not reached any decision as to where I should go. It was awful having to leave Emma and Louise just before Christmas, but go I must.

While I was having afternoon tea alone by my fire I wondered at not hearing from Charles. Certainly it would not be easy for him to reply to my letter and get it delivered, but no doubt Lucy's brother could reverse the procedure I had used. All sorts of fantasies began to worry me then. Was Lucy so trustworthy? Supposing she had taken my letter straight to Greville, or he seeing it in her hand had snatched it away?

But my fantasies were abruptly deferred as the housekeeper, usually reasonably calm and self-possessed, rushed into my room, wringing her hands in utter confusion.

'Miss Abigail, miss, Mr. McClure has called to see you.'

For a moment I thought I must be so feverish that my hearing was playing tricks on me, but a glance at the distraught Mrs. Thwaites told me that I had heard correctly.

'Charles—here?'

'You best wrap up, miss, and come down.'

She smothered me with two of my heaviest shawls and shakily I allowed her to help me down the forbidding staircase, to find Emma standing in the hall talking to Charles.

'My dearest Abbey,' Charles began, coming to the foot of the stairs to reach out to me. 'I was so distressed to hear that you are not well. How are you feeling?'

I went willingly to his outstretched arms.

The heavy oak door slammed shut with a threatening interruption, and we all turned to see Greville standing just inside, tapping his boots with his riding crop.

'Better it would seem,' he said in a loud voice. 'So, *Mr.* McClure, you can take your wench from under *my* roof.'

# *Twelve*

CHARLES had his arm round my shoulders, and I felt the pressure of his fingertips as he endeavoured to restrain himself.

'I've come to do just that,' he said, 'and also . . .' he glanced to where Mrs. Thwaites was hovering on the bottom stair.

Greville followed his gaze.

'All right, Thwaites,' he said brusquely, 'you've heard enough to pass on to the gossips, that will be all.' He swished his riding crop after her as she crossed the large hall and disappeared through the door leading to the stairs and servants' quarters.

'I've also come to talk with you, Greville,' Charles said.

'We've nothing to talk about—but you'd better come into the drawing room. Never let it be said that I didn't offer hospitality even to a McClure.'

Emma was looking pale, and, I noticed, trembling a little as we moved into the drawing room.

Charles insisted that I sit by the fire while he stood behind my chair gallantly protecting me.

Greville closed the door firmly. For once he appeared not to be the worse for drink, and now seeing the two men together Greville was little different in height or stature to Charles, except that Charles had the more classic figure, no doubt due to his military training.

'I hope for old times' sake, Greville,' Charles went

on, 'we can talk man to man without animosity, and I must begin by apologising for Abbey's behaviour. She was only trying to help me, but it is now very obvious that you were the person to take the papers from Edward's person, and because you have destroyed them it is equally obvious that they were in my favour, as Edward indicated to his wife.'

'You have no proof of any of these accusations, and you had no business to implicate my sister-in-law. My office and all its contents are my private belongings, no one has the right to pry into my affairs.'

'I have apologised already,' Charles replied curtly. 'Now I think you owe Abbey an apology. There was no need to leave her locked in a cold, draughty room all night.'

Greville glanced across at me and grinned, and I inwardly shrank from his obnoxious inference. He turned back to Charles, still grinning.

'You never did like the way I treated my women, did you, Charles?'

Both Emma and I looked from one man to the other in bewilderment. They were talking almost like old friends.

'We're a lot older now, Grev, and I would hope a lot wiser. I've come to take Abbey away. She will be staying with Hannah until after Christmas, while we make plans to visit her family as soon as we can. We hope to be married at the very earliest opportunity. Meanwhile it is my belief that you and I should come to some understanding.'

'Understanding?' Greville roared. 'I do not share your belief, sir!'

'For the sake of your wife, and Abbey, and for our children, the future generation, Grev, please, I beg you, let us not continue with this useless feud. Surely we can put an end to his nonsense which has provided the locals with gossip for over a century.'

'You seek to be above yourself, Charles,' Greville said, angrily. 'Just as you always did. A military title does not give you the right to own everything within your grasp.'

'Greville, you know perfectly well I do not seek to own anything which is not mine. But the monastery ruins and land I believe to be part of the McClure estate. The stone wall is and always has been your boundary on the east side, with the woods to the north, but I am willing to sell you the actual ruins and ground upon which they stand.'

'Sell—to me?' Greville banged his fist hard upon the table, and leaned aggressively towards Charles, who remained quite calm. 'You have an infernal insolence,' Greville scowled.

'I'm sorry you think that. We could, I am sure, come to some agreement over a fair price—after all, the land there is of little use, the ruins unsafe. Only you with your nocturnal business can find a use for it.'

Greville raised his fist, beside himself with anger. Charles held up a restraining hand.

'I beg you, Greville, kindly remember we have ladies present. We are not boys now.'

'Ladies!' Greville sneered. 'Some lady you've chosen for yourself—you're welcome to that one.' He nodded in my direction, and walked across to the window, stuffing his hands in his pockets in an attempt to control his anger.

Emma was beginning to snivel loudly.

Charles went to her with great compassion.

'My dear Mrs. Bond, please—I must ask you to forgive me. Abbey and I at least expected to have your blessing. I'm sorry that my visit here has caused such distress.' Then he turned to me. 'Abbey, my dear go and get your things, I'm taking you to the cottage. It will be best for everyone, you do see that, don't you?'

I stood up. 'Yes, Charles, and thank you.'

Tears were not so very far away as I hurried from the room with Emma close behind.

The two men were left alone and I was curious as to what passed between them, but Charles would tell me nothing as we later left together in his carriage.

'Charles,' I said, 'you and Greville were talking like old friends, calling each other by Christian names?'

He smiled at me, and in his own charming exclusive way kissed me lightly on my cheek.

'I can see that I shall never be able to hide anything from you, Abbey. I pray that I shall never want to. It is probably difficult for you to understand, or imagine us as boys together, but that's how it was.'

'Then why should it have changed, you are both still the same people?' I urged.

Charles was thoughtful, and his expression became grave.

'We were both sent to different schools, and—I suppose inevitably became different people. That is the sad part of growing up. We did remain friendly for a little while even after I went into the military. Then after a spell of duty abroad I came home to be shunned, ignored. I had done nothing and could see no reason for it until my father explained that it was expected of the two families to be at loggerheads.'

'It is too ridiculous,' I said, in exasperation.

Charles shrugged. 'Yes, but the Bonds don't see it like that. Castle Grange is much older than Lyme Towers and they believe they have the statutory rights to be the dominating family of Castle Rock. The McClures have never sought to have precedence over anyone. All we want is to have our land back and be able to lie in peace.'

'I suppose being in the Army hasn't helped your position here?'

'Not really, but, you see, that is the McClure tradition. Every man must have a military career. My father remained a soldier until his late fifties, by which time the estate had already suffered from neglect. Then the worry of getting sufficient labour and the upkeep of the families contributed to his ill-health.'

'But you seem to have willing workers on the estate now, Charles.'

'Most of them inherited families, Abbey. To keep their jobs the men must promise that their lads will become stable hands at the age of twelve years. This is the case on all large farming estates. I don't care for the arrangement. A young man should be free to work for whom he chooses, and not bound by his forefathers' heritage. I do have some loyal workers all the same, and I am grateful, but I would never stand in the way of some brilliant young fellow who wished to go off on some different career. One only does one's best at the job one loves.'

'But you gave up your chosen career in the Army, Charles, and that was the job you loved, was it not?

He looked down at me and smiled again.

'Because I met you,' he said softly.

'But you hadn't met me, Charles, not when you decided to come home to Lyme Towers.'

'Perhaps it was a premonition then, that I was to meet the only woman in the world who could bring me happiness.'

I looked away from him.

'I hope I can give you happiness, Charles,' I whispered. 'You deserve it more than anyone.'

The carriage door opened. We had arrived at what

was to be my new home for a while, and after lowering the carriage steps Reuben helped me to alight.

As we went inside, Charles held my arm.

'I wish with all my heart that I had been taking you to Lyme Towers as my wife, Abbey darling. But we are obliged to wait; even so, you must come up to the house often with Hannah. At least your arrival here will put an end to the gossip concerning Hannah and myself.'

'I'm afraid my leaving Castle Grange like this will provide more for the gossips, though,' I said sadly.

'In a small village such as ours, my dear,' Charles said, drily, 'when there isn't any gossip, the locals will soon invent some.'

My bags were taken to my room, and Charles took his leave.

'I hope your sister wasn't too distressed, Abbey?' Hannah said, as we sat by the fire.

'She wailed noisily as she is prone to do,' I told Hannah. "It is a wrench to leave her and the baby and just before Christmas, but after what happened I could not stay at Castle Grange. Of course, Emma didn't know that I was even locked in Greville's room, let alone what took place there. Greville made advances and suggestions to me of a most improper nature, Hannah, and I had to struggle with him. I have not spoken of it to anyone save Mrs. Thwaites, who came to my rescue, and would beg you not to mention it to Charles. Emma cannot suspect the vulgarity of her own husband, and *she* had the audacity to be constantly warning *me* against Charles.'

'But why, Abbey?' What has your sister against Charles?'

I hesitated. 'Emma thought . . .' I began, then paused. 'that you and Charles—and she was afraid I was going to get hurt,' I blurted.

Hannah laughed. 'Your sister was not alone in thinking that, my dear. But soon, when you and Charles become engaged officially, everyone will know how wrong they were.'

Talking freely with Hannah, and now able to see Charles so much more frequently, took away the sting of leaving Emma, and before many days had passed a letter was awaiting me at Lyme Towers from her, delivered secretly by Lucy's brother.

Lucy, only seventeen, and her brother Tom, the fair-haired youth of fourteen I had encountered before, proved to be trustworthy servants. No doubt, they and their widowed mother who lived in the village with several younger children derived much amusement from the intrigue learned from Lucy and Tom, each working in the opposing big houses.

A regular correspondence was soon in operation between Emma and me, which gave us some comfort, but I worried constantly on Emma's behalf. I could never wholly disregard that night in Greville's room, and his unsavoury advances towards me. Nor could I believe that it was an isolated incident. How many mistresses was he keeping? Mrs. Thwaites had assured me he would never harm Emma, but I was not fully convinced.

There were adjustments to be made now in my new way of life, for although the servants from Lyme Towers looked after Hannah's needs, and the cottage, there were numerous tasks she preferred to do for herself, and naturally I did my share.

But our days were filled mostly with visits to the big house. When Charles could spare the time from his estate duties we would ride together, and during the long winter evenings he showed me over Lyme Towers, and we enjoyed making many new plans for the future. When he was not at home I worked with

Hannah, looking through dusty ledgers, household account books, bills, receipts, even old letters, and the task did not prove as tedious as I had anticipated. Indeed, it became most impressive as I learned much about the McClure family of the previous century.

When either Hannah or myself found some entry or item worthy of recognition we would collaborate and discuss the matter, putting it to one side for Charles's scrutiny, as we did one morning, when after browsing through the oldest of the account books dating back to the sixteen hundreds, I discovered that regular sums of money had been paid to charity.

'Charles's family seem to have been a very good living and generous family, Hannah,' I said. 'It does not seem to befit them to have embarked upon a feud. A monthly contribution of two whole guineas was given to some charitable organisation.'

'But that would have been money they could ill-afford, most likely, Abbey. To whom was the money paid?'

'It does not mention any person or organisation, just: "A charitable cause." But look, it occurs regularly on the last day of each month.'

Hannah left her ledgers and came to look over my shoulder. I turned the pages quickly as each month we saw the same entry recorded.

'How strange,' she mused. 'And it continued for many months.'

'Years,' I corrected. 'The first date upon which it is entered is towards the end of 1665, and it continued until 1703, unless a later book is missing.'

'Now that date should signify something, I'm sure, but what?' Hannah stroked her chin thoughtfully.

'Perhaps Charles will know—hark, that is Humphrey barking, a welcoming bark, so Charles has probably just come in,' I said, opening the door to find Charles removing his coat in the hall.

I ran eagerly to him, anxious to discuss the matter, but he caught me in his arms and pressed his lips to mine.

'Oh, Abbey,' he said, exerting his manly strength in a bear-like hug. 'It's so good to have you here to greet me when I come in.'

'Charles, dear,' I urged, 'do come and see these old books. Tell us about your ancestors, were they very wealthy?'

Charles laughed. 'I shouldn't think so—why?'

We joined Hannah and explained to Charles the reason for our interest.

'Mm . . . 1703,' Charles repeated, slowly. 'That was the year of the terrible storm—I know of no other great family events, but, of course, that is a long way back. Several generations in fact.'

'It is amazing that you still have all these old books and papers, Charles,' I said.

'I found them in an old unused attic, in a tin trunk. I doubt that my father knew they were here. That's how Edward and I began our searching—perhaps, though, it would have been better if I had burnt the lot without delving into the past—I'm sorry, Hannah, my dear.'

Glancing at Hannah, I noticed that she was actually wiping the corner of her eye, and I felt no jealousy as Charles put his arm round her.

'Really I am,' he said, softly. 'But if we ever discover what lies behind all this mistrust we shall be proud of Edward. His keen eye certainly found something—maybe I am thoroughly stupid not to see further revealing information.'

'Where was Edward searching, Charles?' I asked.

'He hadn't started on the books you and Hannah

have there. There were copies of legal papers tied in bundles. Mostly to do with the deeds of the house and cottages on the estate.

'Charles,' I asked, hesitantly, 'What makes you *so* sure that the monastery ruins and land were once owned by the McClures?'

'I'm not absolutely sure, Abbey, and must confess it is only hearsay passed on from father to son down through the years to excuse this ridiculous dispute.

Hannah had quietly sat down again at the large table and was comparing the household account book that I had been examining with the huge ledgers.

'Another strange entry, Charles,' she said, 'is the constant repair to the Lodge.'

'Yes, Edward noticed that on some receipts, but we assumed that either the Lodge was demolished, or was the name given to one of the cottages. The possible one being yours, Hannah, as it stands alone.'

'No, no.' Hannah said, quickly. 'There was a large sum spent on the roof slating in January 1681. Our cottage is thatched.'

'Yes, so it is.' Charles took a closer look. 'It all quite baffles me, but, you see, the whole estate may have looked quite different one hundred and fifty years ago. Come along, you have spent enough time worrying your heads over this. I insist that all this be left now until the New Year. Tomorrow is Christmas Eve, and I'm sure you both have things to do for yourselves. How about Reuben taking you both into Exeter to see the shops?'

Hannah and I exchanged glances.

'I'm enjoying working here,' I said. 'I have no shopping to do, but if Hannah . . .'

Hannah laughed. 'I have no such inclination either. My dear Charles, you have started us on a search and we refuse to give up. Perhaps, though, a day or two of rest over the Christmas, Abbey?'

'Remember that you are both to spend Christmas Day here with me, after we have attended morning service,' Charles said.

'And on Boxing Day I am to be your hostess at the cottage, so that all your servants can have a well-deserved holiday with their families,' Hannah said.

'That sounds a splendid arrangement,' I agreed, 'but you must have lots of baking to do, Hannah, so I shall help you.'

'Tomorrow will be a busy day for me,' Charles said, with satisfaction. 'I have slaughtered the bullock in readiness for me to visit each family on the estate tomorrow with the apportionate share of one pound to each head in family. That means I shall be working all day. You are welcome to come with me, Abbey.'

I gave the matter a little thought before declining.

'Next year might be different,' I said shyly.

'Next year, my dearest, you will be obliged to accompany me as my wife.'

Hannah's delicate lips parted in a rare, tender smile. She inclined a slight nod in my direction, perhaps a trifle enviously as she left the room.

Charles immediately encircled me in his fond embrace . . .

The next morning I helped Hannah with some baking, glad that my mother had insisted upon both Emma and myself taking a course of lessons from a renowned French chef, for, as she so often remarked, you could not command a high standard of cuisine in your own kitchen unless you yourself had a certain degree of knowledge upon the subject.

After luncheon Hannah decided to go the the village and afterwards to the churchyard with some holly, so

I walked part way with her, then returned through the estate.

Passing the stables, I couldn't resist visiting Silver Quest, where I found Tom grooming her.

As soon as I spoke to Silver Quest she became excited, obviously thinking I had come to take her out.

'She's missing our daily ride, Tom,' I said, patting the filly's nose.

'I was just wondering, miss, whether I oughtn't to go for canter on her meself. She's quite restless without Duke, she knows the master's gone without her.'

I had become very attracted to my lively mare.

'Well, I've nothing else to do,' I asserted. 'I'll take her across the meadows myself.'

'Oh.' Tom's face fell. 'Is that wise, miss?'

'I can handle Silver Quest, Tom. I've been out riding every day since I came to the cottage,' I assured him.

'But not without the master, miss.'

'Saddle her up for me, Tom, and don't worry. Just a gentle ride round for exercise, and we'll soon be back.

It didn't take long for me to choose the bridle-path I should take. I longed to see Emma and Louise again, so rode along close to the boundary stone wall, taking care to keep to the McClure side, but looking for the best vantage point to view Castle Grange.

It was no good suggesting that Emma should meet me here. She was hopeless at walking anywhere, and if she suddenly started going out for fresh air, Greville would surely suspect. On her last note she had promised to visit the cottage if and when Greville went to Exeter. But no doubt if he went he would insist she went too, knowing that at the first opportunity we should meet.

The only part visible were the chimneys and turrets of Castle Grange, which looked sinister against the skyline. It was indeed a very old mansion house, probably dating back to the fourteenth century, and now, with the meadows on the headland wearing their winter rusty apparel, the little I could see of the cliff-side house appeared bleakly isolated.

The sea was rough, the waves far below crashing loudly on the shingle, and I found myself looking down at the old monastery ruins, more visible now with many of the trees bare. The surrounding land from the valley to the headland stretched open in its vastness. How could anyone be certain to whom it belonged?

Charles was so convinced, no doubt because it skirted his land, but being adjacent to the Bond estate, why shouldn't Greville be equally convinced?

But then, as Charles said, if a Bond had proof they could stake a legitimate claim, and would have done so long since.

Silver Quest began pawing the ground, and tossing her head, but I was quite happy to sit and reflect, so that I did not notice the black menacing clouds gathering, or the wind rising as the December dusk descended.

Only when my skirts began to blow did I realize how long I had been there, and suddenly, as a tremendous moaning wind caught at my cape and lifted my bonnet, Silver Quest reared up throwing me to the ground.

Stunned, confused, I was forced to remain still as black emptiness closed in upon me, and I heard the thud of my filly's hooves getting fainter, and fainter . . .

# *Thirteen*

IT COULD ONLY HAVE BEEN a momentary blackout, but as I struggled to my feet I could see what had frightened Silver Quest.

At the cliff edge stood the monk, and once more he was beckoning to me.

Ordinarily I would have believed myself to be concussed, but he had a manner so gentle, like Charles, and from past encounters I was not afraid any more of the ghost.

'It's too late!' I cried. 'It's growing dark and I've lost my horse. I cannot go with you now.'

'Come, Abbey,' he said in a rich soothing voice.

'Only for a little while—for the last time. I can show you where the truth lies hidden. Come, child—then I can be at peace, peace . . .'

His voice trailed, his figure looked shadowy in the fading light, but instinctively I went towards him, giving no thought as to whether I was hurt or not.

Along the remainder of the stone wall to the cliff edge, clutching tightly at my billowing skirts, I followed the ghostly monk down the narrow cliff path where I had come up on my escapade previously. Just as on that night he was always a little ahead of me, just out of reach, but now I hurried on after him, fearing nothing except when I looked down to the rocks and the clouds of foam and spray from the breakers on the shore.

After reaching the shingle beach he disappeared

through the natural doorway of rock. I pursued cautiously, noticing the wet shingle, and distinctive salty smell.

Now at last I was really in the heart of the ruins. Shingle, rock and bricks all combined to make a mountain of rubble over which I scrambled, until I followed the monk into what had once been a doorway, down some rough stone steps slippery in places with seaweed, passing underground but going away from the direction of the sea.

This, I thought, must have been the cellars of the old house, which rambled on divided by low narrow archways leading from one to the other, and I had to stoop very low to pass through, but I did notice that barrels and crates were stored there. No wonder Greville was so anxious to own the ruins!

It was like a maze, and the smell was dank, making me feel quite ill, yet still I trailed the monk, until quite suddenly he seemed to have vanished. I realised that I had come to the end, for no doorway led from this room, but to my right the walls were crumbling away and a flight of roughly hewn steep steps led upwards, and I could see the daylight filtering through beyond.

The monk was on the rubble at the top of the steps.

'Come, Abbey, quickly—the tide is coming in. You must reach my dormitory first, and all will be well.'

I held my skirts higher now to protect them from the mud, and after reaching the top step had to pause for breath, and looking about me could only gasp with surprise.

I was standing on a narrow ledge, once a dividing wall, presumably to the monk's dormitory. I recognised this as being the same place where Charles and I had stood looking down at the sea pouring in, but we had been on the opposite side of the room.

Now I had entered from the beach side. Already the sea was lapping back into the room below me, and with horror I realised that there was no going back the way I had come. The tide would be sealing that way off right now.

I glanced round for some means of getting out, but this meant going along the narrow ledge to get to the old doorway where Charles and I had stood before.

The monk seemed to be fading further away now, silhouetted against the dusk. Fear gripped me.

'Fancy bringing me here,' I said angrily. 'I shall fall and be drowned!'

'No, Abbey,' he said kindly, with a voice which immediately assuaged my anger. 'Have no fear. Reach round the ledge a little to your right, where you will find a hole in the wall. It used to be a fireplace. In it I had my mother's trinkets in her workbox. Take it—quickly—while you can still reach it.'

As I watched him he seemed to be disappearing; the wind screamed and the waves crashed ferociously, when suddenly strong arms grabbed me round my waist.

I had felt myself drawn forward, as if trying to reach out to the monk as he vanished, but the arms held me fast. I wanted to cry out, but a hand was clapped over my mouth.

'No be afraid, missie—Oliver got you.'

I allowed myself to go limp in his grasp. The big Virginian Negro, Charles's cook whom I had never met, had somehow followed me. I was so relieved that I almost forgot the monk's request.

Oliver had removed his hand from my mouth when he realised that I had no intention of struggling, but we were in a perilous predicament, the ledge hardly wide enough for me to stand alone, without the added strain of Oliver's huge frame.

'Oliver,' I whispered, 'thank goodness you came, but I must get the box.'

'Box, missie?'

'Yes, didn't you hear the monk—the ghost?'

'I don't saw no one but you, missie, and I take you home to the master,' he said firmly.

'Yes, yes, but first I must get the box. Look, Oliver, hold my hand while I reach out this way—there should be a hole in the wall somewhere.'

'But, missie, this ledge, no safe, we both be drowned —the tide, it coming in.'

'Yes, I know, Oliver, but I can't give up now, I just can't! I *must* find the box.'

'You come back 'nother day, missie. When Master come too,' he offered kindly.

'Oh, Oliver, if only I could make you understand. Please— just hold on to me.'

I still had my back to the poor man, who obviously thought I was mad, but I managed to edge a little farther away, holding tightly to his arm with my right hand.

Evidently he sensed what I was trying to do as I stretched out my left hand groping and feeling along the wall for a hole.

'Me find something,' he said. 'Me stronger than Missie.'

He let go of my right hand and with great agility turned himself round on the ledge, then pressing his massive body against mine he slid his long arm up and down the wall, his nimble fingers searching.

'I don't find nothing, missie. Look, let me get you to safe place, then I come again.'

'But it's getting dark and already the spray is soaking us. Try once more, please, Oliver,' I begged.

There was a deathlike hush, even the sea seemed

to stop its tormenting roar for a moment as I felt Oliver straining and inching his way round me to reach farther along the ledge.

'Ah—ah!' His deep voice boomed through the ruins. 'Hole in the wall, like Missie say. Ah, here is something.'

'Now careful, Oliver,' I said. 'Let me give you more room. I think—yes, now that I have turned round I can get along the ledge by myself, back to the doorway.'

I turned my head now towards the only means of escape, and almost cried with relief as the glow of a lantern became visible, drawing nearer through the old doorway.

But I had to get to that doorway, and so did Oliver, bearing my precious find.

The little twinkle of light from someone's lantern grew larger, then disappeared, before reappearing, and now I could hear the welcoming murmur of distant voices. Fortunately, my rescuers were not as close as I supposed, but coming down the headland towards the Monk's Chapel, so that I was forced to grope my own way inch by inch along the ledge. If they had suddenly come upon me the light could have dazzled my eyes, and in the excitement I might have stumbled and fallen several feet into the room below on the rubble where the sea was seeping its way in.

Somehow sufficient light remained for me to see the ledge, and there was enough of the wall left to hold on to, so that I was able to gather speed and soon reached the doorway.

'Oliver,' I called back. 'Have you got it? Can you manage? If you like you can throw the box to me now.'

There was no answer, so I quickly stepped out through the doorway to safety, but turned to peer back into the dusk for Oliver.

He was so close I jumped back.

'Me safe too, Missie. Carry box on head. Much practice!' and he laughed.

Then a voice came from behind us.

'Abbey—Oliver—where are you?'

I ran towards the lantern, letting my skirts, which I had been clutching tightly, fly in the wind.

'Charles, Charles, we're safe, it's all right,' I said, flinging myself against him, half laughing, half crying with relief.

'Abbey, what do you mean by coming here alone? What madness possessed you?'

'Charles, dear, don't be angry,' I pleaded earnestly. 'I only came out to give Silver Quest some exercise. The monk frightened her and she bolted—oh dear, I do hope she's safe.'

Charles held me fast as if he was afraid to release me again.

'She's back at the stables now,' he said. 'Oliver found her galloping wildly near the house. He managed to catch and calm her, then took her back to the stables where Tom explained that you'd been out on her. Tom was very frightened then, but came looking for me, but meanwhile Oliver met Hannah coming back from the village and she suggested you might be at the ruins.'

'I'm sorry if I frightened everyone,' I said, 'but look, Charles, the monk told me where he'd hidden his mother's box, and Oliver was able to reach it. There's a hole in that wall round the other side, where a fireplace once stood. That must have been Francis Drummond's room and he kept the box in the fireplace. Maybe we shall find some answers in that box.'

Charles wasn't really taking in what I was prattling on about, but staring beyond me. I turned to see Oliver transferring the box from his head to his shoulder.

'You really found that in the wall?' Charles asked incredulously.

'Yes, sir,' Oliver said, his white teeth gleaming happily. 'Box dirty, green with damp. Me take home to clean.'

'I can hardly believe it, but it's dark now, let's get back to the house where we can take a closer look.'

Hannah was anxiously watching for some sign of us, and as we approached the cottage she ran out to meet us. Excitedly I repeated my adventure, as I had just related it to Charles, while Oliver made an attempt to clean the box enough for us to handle.

Wih a mixture of relief and elation I quickly discarded my bonnet and cloak and went to the fire for a warm. Charles brought the box into the parlour and placed it on the hearth.

'Abbey, please, don't ever go off by yourself like that again. Supposing Silver Quest had taken off in the other direction, we should never have known where you were. You might have been seriously injured.'

'Charles, I had no idea that such a thing was about to happen.'

'It mustn't happen again,' he said firmly. 'The ruins are unsafe. You could have been trapped there by the incoming tide. No one ventures through the doorway over the shore.'

'There will be no need for me to go again. The monk begged me to go with him for the last time.'

'But that might have been your untimely end, my dear.'

I smiled at Charles's concern.

'No, I know the monk now. He would never cause me harm—he wants to be at peace, and now that we have found what he wanted us to find, he has gone to his eternal retreat.'

Charles sighed and looked despairingly at Hannah who had prepared tea.

'Charles dear,' she said. 'Let this be a lesson to you. When Abbey sets her mind to do a thing, nothing will stop her.'

'Let's hope, then, that there are no other ghosts to lure her off seeking adventure,' Charles said, laughing.

He remained at the cottage for tea and then returned to Lyme Towers, leaving Hannah and me eagerly attempting to open the box.

As it began to dry we could see that it was made of superior walnut wood, inlaid with a fine mother-of-pearl design, and it was securely locked, the mechanism rusted through, but we eventually managed to prise it open with the help of the long, brass poker.

Inside was a leather bag pulled up tightly at the opening with a drawstring. In it we found a few old coins, a brooch and several trinkets, but nothing of much value or interest, and I felt somewhat disappointed.

The lid of the box was lined with silk, now mildewy and smelling mouldy, so it still wasn't particularly pleasant to handle, and I quickly replaced it in the hearth. As it dried the wood creaked a little, and suddenly a tray from the lid fell out, and there beneath the tray was a bundle of old letters.

The fine vellum had turned yellow, the ink faded but not entirely invisible, so that the name 'Agnes Drummond', written on the top envelope, could easily be read.

The writing was elegant in style and penned with a fine quill, and I felt it was vaguely familiar.

Hannah took the bundle from me and I turned over the envelope I was holding to see if the seal was broken.

It was broken, but had been done with care so

that now after years of being pressed flat it looked intact again, and I recognised it at once.

' "M" for McClure—Charles's seal,' I gasped.

Hannah quickly pulled the next one from the bundle, and the next one, and so on, and all bore the McClure seal.

We were too stunned to speak our thoughts aloud, so grateful that Charles chose that moment to return to the cottage as he always did around nine o'clock.

Usually Hannah would slip quietly off to bed, leaving us alone to enjoy these cherished moments of intimacy, which were becoming increasingly difficult to control as passion burned within us. Charles's dark eyes had a way of exploring mine, as if asking a question there was no need to answer, and we had only to stand in close proximity for me to feel the frenzied desire of his emotion.

But not tonight. Tonight was different, and he must have sensed the excitement of discovery as he stood in the doorway of the little parlour, puzzled at our silence.

'Well, don't look so disappointed that there was no fortune,' he began with a laugh. 'You surely didn't expect . . ?' He stopped as he caught sight of the envelopes. 'What's this—my seal?'

'Yes, Charles,' I said. 'The McClure family seal. What can it mean? This box belonged to Agnes Drummond, see, the letters are addressed to her.'

'Still readable after all these years?' Charles said. 'We'll soon find out. Look inside, Abbey, read the letter.'

'I hardly like to, Charles. They were Agnes's private letters, it doesn't seem honest.'

'But we must surely, if we're to know the truth, he said. 'Why else would your ghost have insisted you found the box?'

'Not *my* ghost, Charles dear,' I said, with a smile. 'The ghost of Francis Drummond.'

'It seems he wanted you to know the truth, darling, so I suggest you read with all haste.'

Hesitantly I pulled the folded letter from the envelope, and read aloud as much of it as I could decipher. The signature at the end was very clear: 'From your ever loving, Alistair.'

The message he had written on that day, dated 1685, was to offer consolation to Agnes, who was distressed that her son Francis, having learned of his illegitimacy, had decided to enter an abbey and become a monk. Alistair McClure begged her forgiveness that he could not marry her so that she and their son could take their rightful place at Lyme Towers, but he already had a legitimate son to follow in his footsteps.

'So one of my ancestors was responsible for poor Agnes's plight,' Charles said.

'But that does not signify very much,' I said. 'The house belonged to Agnes, so, after the storm, and death of Francis, who should have inherited the land? Surely there must have been relatives on her side?'

Charles read the letter again, giving the matter much thought.

'Abbey, the old fisherman with whom you talked the other day on the beach, didn't he say something about Agnes Drummond being a kitchen maid?'

'Yes, that's right, he did.'

'Then it's unlikely that the house belonged to her.'

The letters were tied in a neat bundle with narrow ribbon, and as soon as I tried to untie it the ribbon fell to pieces, rotten with age.

'Go on, Abbey,' Charles urged, 'look through them —who knows what we may learn?'

'But they were written by a far distant grandfather of your, Charles,' I said, somehow apprehensive now of what discovery we were about to make. 'You take them.'

Hannah had been rubbing the old box with a soft duster and brushing the inside when she discovered another tray at the bottom of the box. She managed to lift it out and there she found more letters tied in a bundle.

Charles became almost as excited as a small boy as he drew his chair nearer the fire, and eagerly Hannah and I watched as he searched through the letters.

But these were later ones, addressed to Francis Drummond, but written by the same elegant hand. Amongst them was a copy of a legal document drawn up by a lawyer in Exeter, stating that the Lodge was to be used by Agnes Drummond and her son Francis for the period of their lifetime, after which it would be restored to its natural state, that of being part of the McClure estate, the date of the signatures being December 31st, 1665.

'So, the old monastery was formerly known as the Lodge,' Charles said. 'And most likely it was a similar document to this which Edward found.'

'And which Greville took and destroyed,' I added with bitterness, 'knowing full well that the land and the ruins are yours, Charles.'

Charles fell silent, and a puzzled frown appeared on his face.

'At least now it can be made legally public that it belongs to the McClure estate,' he said, 'and the mystery surrounding Agnes and her son put down. I'm afraid my ancestors were not of such good repute, Abbey—are you still quite sure you wish to marry me?'

'Oh, Charles, it doesn't alter you,' I said, fondly. 'We don't know all the circumstances yet—perhaps there are more skeletons to be unearthed.'

'I must say I have a strong desire to read all the letters, and hope that the poor misguided Agnes, and indeed her son Francis, would not object to my curiosity, but I think we should begin at the beginning. Turn the bundle over, Abbey, so that we take the oldest first. They have been carefully preserved here, just as they were received.'

And so, as Christmas Eve chimed its way into Christmas morn, Charles and I, with Hannah's help, pieced together the fascinating story of Agnes Drummond and her lover Alistair McClure.

The very first letter was a polite note asking if Agnes had recovered from her unsavoury encounter with some ruffians outside the Castle Inn.

It seemed that Alistair McClure was passing through the village on horseback at the time, for he wrote: 'I am indeed pleased that I could be of service to you, and hope the manner in which those lay-abouts felt my riding crop taught them a lesson. When I last visited my brother-in-law at Castle Grange I spoke strongly to him concerning sending a young lady on an errand after dark, and feel sure that Mr. Bond will be more kindly disposed to you in the future.'

Charles's voice faded, all trace of amusement vanished as he looked intently at me.

'Alistair McClure . . .' he muttered.

'Visited his brother-in-law at Castle Grange,' I continued.

'Which means,' Hannah reiterated, 'that Alistair must have married a Bond.'

'Then you and Greville are distant cousins!' I expounded.

# Fourteen

DESPITE THE FACT that the letters spanned some twenty years, we were able to re-create some sort of pattern in the life of Alistair McClure, for he poured out his life story to the little kichen maid, whose sympathetic nature soon promoted her to the status of becoming his mistress.

While serving in the Civil War he had come south from Scotland, and, falling in love with the beautiful Elizabeth Bond, married her, and bought the neighbouring estate to Castle Grange.

When he inherited all the money from his family estate in Scotland he made a present to Elizabeth of the grand mansion he had specially built to his own design, and away from the sea, calling it Lyme Towers, so that for some while the old house, already showing signs of subsidence, remained empty.

Alistair wrote in glowing terms of his beloved wife, Elizabeth, who bore him three sons, but who died in childbirth. He then became a lonely, bitter man when during the year 1665 his eldest two sons, serving in the Army in London, both fell victims of the Plague.

By this time had had met Agnes, who in some measure helped to fill his empty life, the younger son of sixteen being away at military school, when Francis was born.

It was then that Alistair repaired the old house by the sea for his mistress and illegitimate son, and called it the Lodge.

Most of his letters to Agnes had been written prior to her taking up residence at the Lodge, the remaining few spread out over many years presumably because he visited her frequently at the Lodge.

'Poor Alistair McClure,' I said, at length, 'What a tragic life.'

'But at last we know how it all came about,' Charles said. 'When Agnes committed suicide he helped Francis turn the Lodge into a monastery and paid for the materials so that the monks could build their own church. I suppose after the storm and sad fate of the monks, Alistair was too old to care about his land and setting things in legal order. It seems it has been a bad habit of my family to neglect estate affairs in their declining years. We must search through the old family bible and see if his marriage and death are recorded there.'

They were, as we discovered next day, Christmas Day, after going to early morning service and, while waiting for luncheon to be served at Lyme Towers afterwards, Charles showed Hannah and me a very dilapidated family bible.

'I haven't looked at this since I was a boy,' he said, placing the heavy book on the table. Some pages were torn, or loose, and one of the big clasps broken, but the entries in the front of the book were interesting.

The bible had been given to Alistair McClure on the occasion of his marriage to Elizabeth Bond in 1643 and the birth of his three sons were recorded: Craig —1644, Duncan—1647, and Andrew—1649, when Elizabeth died.

'Fancy you not knowing that the two families were related, Charles,' I said.

'I've never bothered to delve back into our history until recently,' Charles said. 'This old bible seemed of little interest to me as it is so old. The current one was given to my grandfather when he was married, presumably because this one was well used and full up. In any case, I couldn't see how births, marriages and deaths could solve the mystery of the monastery ruins.'

'Well, it all ties in nicely now. Obviously the sum of money Alistair paid to charity was really Agnes's keep. We must go and tell Emma and Greville. Do you think Greville knows that he is distantly related to you?'

Charles shrugged. 'Shall we ever discover what he thinks or knows? Like me he has probably had little interest in such ancient family history. One thing is certain, and that is that he took the documents from Edward's body, and hoped no one would ever find out the truth. But we have, and this means we can end the dispute. Though my family are not altogether without blame, so—I have been thinking—I will make a peace offering to Greville of the monastery ruins—the rest of the land is, as I thought, mine.'

'Oh, Charles, how generous of you!'

'Let's hope Greville will think so,' Charles muttered.

After enjoying our Christmas dinner Charles and I set off in the carriage. Already the rain had started to fall and the wind was rising to gale force.

Castle Grange looked dismally sombre on this grey Christmas Day as we approached it, the horses slowing their pace as they mounted the incline toward the cliff edge.

From the carriage window we could see the mountainous waves plundering the shore as we turned off into the grounds.

'An angry sea, to be sure,' Charles said, 'and by the heavy sky there's more to come.'

As soon as the carriage rolled to a standstill close

to the shelter of the solid oak doors, Charles left me and pulled the bellrope.

There was no answer to his summons, so he pulled a second time. The grey stone walls held no more appeal for me now, but looked aggressively forbidding. Charles glanced towards me in the carriage, so I anxiously peered from the open window.

'Is it possible they are away for Christmas?' he asked. 'Or perhaps gone to friends for the day?'

'Emma hasn't mentioned any such arrangements,' I told him. 'Try just once more—Mrs. Thwaites should be there.'

Charles tugged extra hard at the bell and a few seconds later the door moved a little.

It was a white-faced Mrs. Thwaites who peeped cautiously round the door, so I scrambled from the carriage.

'We've come to see Emma and Greville,' I said, 'with good news, Mrs. Thwaites.'

She shook her head.

'Not today, Miss Abigail. Begging your pardon, sir, but I can't allow you to step inside today.'

'But why not, Mrs. Thwaites?'

'Mrs. Emma is resting, Miss Abigail—oh, she's not ill, but not quite herself like.'

'And Mr. Bond?' Charles asked.

'Drunk, and in a fearful rage,' she whispered.

'Well, couldn't I run up and see Emma quickly?' I begged.

The door was flung back, almost throwing Mrs. Thwaites off her feet.

Greville stood scowling at us, his eyes red and glazed. The door swung lightly as his heavy frame used it for support, swaying as he tried to keep his balance.

'No, you couldn't see anyone,' he said in a slurring

voice. 'It's Christmas Day, and we're having a good time.'

'Greville,' Charles spoke kindly, 'It's because it is Christmas we've called. Naturally Abbey would like to see her sister, but the important thing is that we've solved all the past mystery, and we hoped that you and Emma and your little daugher too, of course, would come back to Lyme Towers with us to spend the remainder of the day there, so that we can share the good news.'

Greville lurched forward, but managed to regain his hold on the door.

'Get off my land, you thieving scoundrels. Get back to your palace,' and he slammed the door in our faces.

Charles put his arm round me.

'My dear Abbey, I'm sorry. It is no use trying to reason with him in such an ugly mood. Perhaps we can try again tomorrow.'

I wept a little as we journeyed back to Lyme Towers, for Emma, that she should have to spend Christmas with a man like Greville Bond.

I was glad of Charles's strength, and tried not to be too miserable, but the magic of the day was gone.

Hannah and I returned to the cottage quite early; apart from my disappointment at not seeing Emma, we were all tired from being up half the night reading the old letters, so were thankful to get to bed.

The wind howled noisily, the windows and doors of the small cottage rattled ominously on their hinges, but I did eventually drift into a troubled sleep, only to be awakened suddenly by a commanding voice, calling: 'Abbey, Abbey—go to Emma.'

I was off the bed before I was properly awake. My head spun in the darkness, and I realised I had been dreaming.

When I recovered I lit a candle and stood looking

out of the window. I had never seen such a black night, and yet such a noisy one.

A flash of lightning streaked across the sky, followed by the boom of angry thunder.

'Abbey, Abbey—are you awake?'

I knew this was Hannah's voice.

'Yes, Hannah, come in. The storm must have woken us.'

'I thought you called, and told me you were going to fetch Emma and the baby,' she said, with an unconvincing laugh.

Was Hannah sleep-walking?

'Go back to bed, Hannah—you've been dreaming too.'

But she was fully dressed.

'Abbey, dear. The voice was quite clear.'

Another flash, another roll of thunder, and even the ground shook.

'Well, I thought I must have been dreaming, but I too heard someone calling me and they told me to go and fetch Emma and the baby. It seems strange to have both had the same dream.'

'Hark! A horseman! Listen, Abbey! What can anyone be doing out on such a night as this?'

The clip-clop of horse's hooves echoed eerily in the night, and as the wind dropped for a second we could hear the rider at the back of the cottage.

And then a voice below my window.

'Abbey! Abbey! Are you awake?'

'Charles!' I whispered. 'In the middle of the night!'

Hannah was already draping my heavy shawl round my shoulders, and we went down stairs.

Charles stepped just inside the little kitchen, his boots muddy, water dripping from his hat and cloak.

'Can't you sleep either?' he said.

Even in his eyes I could see a fear, so unlike Charles.

'Something's wrong,' he said. 'I don't know what, but I just had to get up and come and see if you were both all right. The ground feels strangely hot, and is vibrating—trees are down, I'm afraid some of the thatches might be struck.'

'Something is wrong at Castle Grange, I know it,' I said, suddenly. 'I wasn't dreaming, nor were you, Hannah. I must go to Emma.'

'Not now, Abbey,' Hannah pleaded. 'You can't go out in this.'

'I must, I must. I'll go and dress at once. You will take me, Charles, please?'

He nodded and I went quickly upstairs.

Duke carried us both, and as we took the short cut along the bridle-path through the woods and the meadows beyond, ear-splitting cracks thundered through the intense, stifling atmosphere, and reaching the grounds of Castle Grange we met servants screaming and running in panic away from Castle Grange.

'The servants' door—I'll go in that way,' I said, as I slid to the ground.

'Everyone make for Lyme Towers,' Charles ordered in a loud voice. 'You'll have shelter there—just get back from the cliff.'

'Oh, Mr. McClure, sir!' a voice cried from the turmoil. 'What a blessing you've come. The master's gone mad. Singing and a shouting at the back there, sir, drunk as a lord, and saying as 'ow he's going to get to the ruins to save his stuff there.'

'All right, Sam, take me to him—we'll calm him, even if I have to use my fists.'

I ran through the house, calling Emma. She was in her room with Louise in her arms, gathering garments of clothing and crying hysterically.

'Emma, Emma, come quickly!' I cried. 'The storm—the sea!'

'What's happening, Abbey? I don't know what to do.'

'Just bring the essentials, there's no time—we must get Louise to safey.'

The thunderous explosion that followed caused us both to get to the floor. Everything in the old house rattled and shook violently.

Mrs. Thwaites clutched at my arm.

'Come away, miss, through the library. The back of the house and part of the garden has gone—gone into the sea.'

The next few hours were indescribable, but we made a miraculous escape through the library into Greville's little room, and out through the narrow door which I discovered led into the cellars and out on to the cliff path which led up to the headland and stone wall.

It was everyone for himself. We had no time to glance back as the sea tore at the cliff behind us, tormenting us with its savage anger.

Dirty, wet and exhausted we at last reached the wall, then groped our way along it with the aid of the lantern Mrs. Thwaites was carrying.

By this time the whole village was awake to the disaster. Lanterns flickered in the darkness. Help came from everywhere as the men joined forces to get the servants and workers on Greville's estate to safety.

Emma, the baby and myself were bundled on to a small farmcart and taken to Lyme Towers.

Oliver had gone to look for Charles, but the maids at Lyme Towers were boiling cauldrons of soup while Hannah distributed it to the victims as they arrived.

Just before dawn as the storm reached its height

the whole earth shook, and people screamed with fright at the deafening roar.

I ran to the balcony of Lyme Towers, which looked towards the sea.

Sam and Oliver, supporting Charles on either side, staggered up the steps.

'Charles, Charles!' I screamed and went to help.

'It's all right, Abbey, thank God you managed to get here to safety,' he stammered. 'I'm not badly hurt . . .'

He reached the top of the steps, and held on to a balcony pillar, his other arm round my shoulders.

A flash of lightning lit up the sky and meadows, and as we glimpsed the remaining turrets of Castle Grange, it toppled and vanished over the cliff edge.

I clutched at Charles as there in the sky the shadow of the monk was poised, briefly, as he blessed us before vanishing.

'Oh, Charles,' I sobbed, and wept bitterly.

'A landslide has taken the lot,' Charles whispered. 'It's a miracle anyone was saved. The coast from Castle Grange to the ruins has vanished.'

'And Greville?' I whispered.

'I couldn't get to him. He fought me off, then the cliff where he was standing just gave way. Sam grabbed my arm and I hung on until Oliver came to help. If only Greville had listened. If only he hadn't been drunk.'

'That wasn't your fault, Charles, dearest. You did all you could. Poor Emma, she has lost very nearly everything. Thank goodness she has Louise, but Greville did so much want a son,' I said.

'He might yet have a son,' a voice murmured behind us. It was Emma who had heard it all. Charles offered her a protective hand, and she pressed it fiercely to her lips as weeping shook her body. 'In the summer,' she sobbed, 'Greville shall have his son.'

We looked at her aghast, and I was angry with myself for not recognising her condition.

'And we'll help to rebuild a new Bond estate, my dear,' Charles was saying. 'We're all one family, after all.'

'And we'll make sure the next generation will be proud of their names,' Emma said, as she turned to go back inside the house.

'Come, my darling,' Charles said to me. 'There is work to do, we must make provision for everyone here.'

But together we paused for a moment, looking towards the sea, where Francis Drummond, the monk, my friendly ghost, had retreated for ever.

A TOWERING MANSION
AND ITS TANGLED LEGACY
OF EVIL AND DESIRE

THE STORMY ROMANTIC SAGA BY

It began with Eustacia, first mistress of Rommany, whose love for Duncan Blackmore was not to be denied. But the innumerable rooms and sins of Rommany drew her into the grip of a sinister plot that spread its evil stain across seven decades....

Until, in the life of Constance, her granddaughter, three generations of mystery converge in a fateful decision to love the hypnotic Leonard, a man cruelly linked to the shadowy past.

Suddenly, the gloom of Rommany is punctuated by ominous thumpings in the night, and Constance must pierce the veil that enshrouds her hopeless passion—so the ultimate secret of Rommany can be unmasked at last!

28340/$1.75

ROM 6-76